COSMOBIOI  S

Sundress Publications • Knoxville, TN

Copyright © 2021 by Jilly Dreadful
ISBN: 978-1-951979-21-8
Library of Congress: 2021938557
Published by Sundress Publications
www.sundresspublications.com

Editor: Saba Razvi
Editorial Assistants: Kanika Lawton, Anna Black, Erin Elizabeth Smith
Editorial Interns: Kathleen Gullion, Abigail Renner, Mary Sims, Ashley Somwaru

Colophon: This book is set in Bembo Std and Tahoma.
Cover Image: Jilly Dreadful
Cover Design: Kristen Ton
Book Design: Tierney Bailey, Erin Elizabeth Smith

COSMOBIOLOGICAL: STORIES
Jilly Dreadful

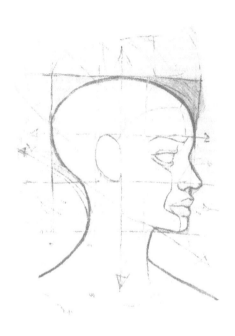

ACKNOWLEDGEMENTS

Some of the stories featured in this collection have appeared previously in other publications. I'd like to thank *Lightspeed Magazine* for taking a chance on a queer love story set at a science summer camp when they published "5x5." *Devilfish Review* was the first home for "The Mermaid Café," and "Mooncakes," was featured in *NonBinary Review* and was nominated for a Pushcart Prize. "De Deabus Minoribus Exterioris Theomagicae," originally appeared in the first all-female Lovecraft anthology, *She Walks in Shadows*, published by Innsmouth Free Press and edited by Silvia Moreno-Garcia and Paula R. Stiles (2015), which won the World Fantasy Award for best anthology. It has been republished by Prime Books as *Cthulhu's Daughters: Stories of Lovecraftian Horror* (2016). My weird little story was long-listed for Best Horror of the Year in 2016 by the legendary editor, Ellen Datlow. "Lost Angeles" originally appeared as "Persephone + Hades" in Rough Magick (2015); KT Ismael helped me workshop the story, and it was edited by Francesca Lia Block and Jessa Marie Mendez and published by Dangerous Angel. My husband, Brad, was integral to helping me revise, "Even the Simulacrum Heart is a Lonely Hunter" when the impairment of my short term memory prevented me from holding the whole story in my mind long enough to fix continuity issues.

CONTENTS

For my mother Jean,
who taught me how to love, so that I might be able to love others.

AN INVOCATION FOR THE WAY SATURN SQUARED NEPTUNE AND FLOODED THE UNIVERSE

Stop me if you've heard this one.

I had this good friend, the planet Neptune; she had taken the form of a mermaid on the other side of the reality fabric. She was variegated with all the shades of blue that could possibly be found on a planet too far away for human investigation, but just far enough away to stoke human curiosity. Shades of blue that swirled in the daylight sky; shades of blue that could only be found in the center of a flame; and shades of blue one might expect to find on the cover of a Neil Gaiman hardcover novel. The collection of these colors formed a mosaic upon the mermaid's tail. Neptune's skin was the kind of blue that sounds like a viola being played on a winter day in the Transylvanian mountains, and her hair was the exact shade of deep blue as the woman you've known since she was a girl.

Even if Neptune had not been languishing in a bright white clawfoot bathtub, everything about Neptune was fluid—from the way her hair was caught in a current of its own and floated in gentle, levitating waves around her shoulders, to the mermaid's mutable, mercurial nature. She often didn't know what she wanted, but she knew what she did not want—and, in the opinion of this humble narrator, one is just as good as the other.

The mermaid craved open waters but was trapped in a bathtub.

There was a knock at the door, and the mermaid bade the visitor to enter, and the embodiment of Saturn in the form of an engineer walked toward Neptune. Saturn was a multitude of golds and beiges, and the colors rotated around his body like storms, shifting his skin tone like clouds heavy with lightning. A ring of asteroids were bound around his head like a crown, yet he carried a red toolbox. He carried himself with the otherworldly grace that comes from an ancient kind of knowing only understood by fellow planets.

Even if Saturn hadn't been wearing a crown made of asteroids, everything about him was planetary royalty—but not the kind of frivolous royalty that starts wars or barters for brides—the kind of royalty that comes from a deeply seeded service to others; the kind of royalty that, if one looked closely enough, held the faintest hints of blue around the edges. Saturn had a poet's soul, but the hands of an engineer; and, if truth be told, he often had a hand in many of the problems that needed fixing. Whether or not he admitted it to Neptune.

When Neptune saw Saturn, she flipped her fishtail and leaned her torso forward against the tub and her blue heart glowed with soft phosphorescence usually reserved for creatures of the deep sea.

"I'll trade you my voice for a pair of legs," Neptune said. "Whaddya say?" She wriggled her eyebrows to really sell the idea.

"Silence is a form of violence," Saturn replied, "I'm not comfortable silencing you."

"You'd be surprised by the forms of violence to which I'm immune," said Neptune, and she leaned back in the tub and flopped her tail with the air of a bored middle schooler. "You know why the sea is salty, right?"

"Why?" asked Saturn.

"Saltwater is made from the tears my people no longer have to shed."

"So," Saturn said, trying to puzzle together the riddles the mermaid spoke in, "you can't cry?"

"You know what happens when a creature can't cry? If you can't cry, others get to thinking that you're immune to everything, and, so, they treat you like you *are* immune to everything. Until, eventually, you do become immune. To every-thing."

Ever the engineer, Saturn offered a possible answer in reply, "You have to teach people the way you want to be treated."

"Yeah, but how do you teach someone to not hurt you if you can't even cry? People don't seem to take things like that seriously otherwise."

"We're not people," Saturn reminded Neptune.

Neptune smiled the kind of smile that made Saturn think of shipwrecks and barnacled treasure chests. "Does that mean you're never gonna make me wish my body could make tears? Are you gonna make me stop wishing I had legs?"

Saturn considered for a moment. "No."

Neptune's eye grew wide with doubt, and she became offended by the truthfulness of his admission. "How could you say such a thing? Don't you love me?"

"I do," Saturn said, and he took out a straight pipe wrench nearly as large as the red toolbox he had brought with him. "And that's why I'm not going to promise those things."

"Wouldn't you rather find a different, more habitable planet, though? One with a great set of legs in the Goldilocks zone?"

"You mean Earth?"

"Well, yeah."

"No."

"No?"

"Yeah."

"Huh," is all Neptune said, then after a beat. "Why not?"

"Darlin'," Saturn said as he knelt beside the bathtub, "because you're the major aspect of my life. There will always be transits in the stars. I'll conjunct other planets. But there's only one Neptune."

And with that, Saturn handed Neptune the wrench.

"I'm afraid," the mermaid said as she cradled the wrench in her hands.

"I know, but," Saturn reached out and held Neptune's left cheek in his right hand, "bathtubs are no substitutes for open water."

"I want you to come with me."

"Sorry," Saturn said. "Can't breathe under water."

"Well," Neptune replied, sitting straighter as she did, "I can't promise it's easy. But it's totally worth learning! I'll teach you how to let the water treat your lungs."

"Deal."

Neptune raised the pipe wrench with both arms and bit her lip. She hesitated a moment and then asked, "You ready?"

"Ready."

And with that, Neptune cracked the bathtub with the pipe wrench and the room instantly flooded with water, until it busted the windows. And then the world filled with water, until it busted the universe.

And the two planets chased each other across the Milky Way. Saturn's constant orbital presence assured Neptune that he wasn't going anywhere. And Neptune taught Saturn how to invite the water to wash over him, breathe deep, and forget to drown.

THE FAUN WITH A FULL MOON HEART

Once upon a time, a shooting star fell in love with the earth, and thus a shooting star child was born beneath a full bloom moon in the form of a satyr girl. When asked, the faun freely admitted that it was great fun being genealogically linked to shooting stars. "But," she'd say, her wide doe eyes shifting back and forth, and her voice lowering to a hush, "shooting stars have the worst road trips: they're always light years too long and there's no proper room for your hooves and hind quarters. I was cooped up in the shooting star for so long, I almost forgot how strong my legs are." Luckily, as soon as her hooves met the earth, her soft brown fur, her felted antlers, and her white polka dot spots became a blur in the forest when her legs remembered what it was to run.

Between the dappled sunlight of the great fir trees, there was a hunter. He was a crack shot if there ever was one, and he cherished the idea of bows and arrows being properly sporting. He was hunting for many things that day in the woods. He was hunting for a meal first and foremost since he was, at heart, a practical man. He was also hunting for music since he had a musician's ear, and he found a symphony in the wind and birdsong. Even though he wasn't directly hunting for love, he wouldn't have protested too much had it crept out from under the underbrush and made itself known.

But one day, while the satyr girl was on a wild run of hers, the hunter mistook her blur for a full-grown meal. He put arrow to string and let the arrow fly.

The hunter had only been looking for a meal, but little did he know he had managed to snag all three things he had been hunting for when his arrow found her.

It struck her in the heart. And though she fell down nearly dead after the arrow pierced her chest—though she was keenly aware of how uncomfortable breathing suddenly had become with the arrow lodged in a such an undesirable location—she was shocked to discover that it was not the end of her.

It was not the beginning of her, either; for being a shooting star child, she had a long and beautifully lit life before the hunter ever arrived on the scene. She had fallen in love with Dionysus for one glorious night when they both were tipsy on an entirely different kind of spirit. She wrote haikus to Artemis and then sang them into existence, breathing life into her words through her own exquisite song magic. In her spare time, the faun knitted together columbine petals and the heads of snapdragons to create clothes for the wood nymphs who wanted to know what it was like to no longer be naked. And though she knew he'd just grow back the next day, our satyr girl plucked Narcissus out of the ground, roots and all, and tossed his bud in the river when he got a little too narcissistic, in the clinical sense, for her taste.

After the arrow pierced her flesh, her heart began to bleed. But being a shooting star child, her blood was made of starlight and resonated at such a pitch and frequency that the bleeding could only be heard by the hunter alone. So, he used his skilled musician ears to track the satyr girl to the thicket she had secluded herself within.

When she realized that she could not remove the arrow herself, the faun came to understand what it was to surrender: to really and truly entrust the care of her heart in the hands of a hunter who promised to leave her heart better than when he found it. He listened to the flutter of her heartbeat particular to her body alone, and then used his string-toughened hands to delicately remove the arrow from the meat of her heart.

And in the process of taking her heart and light in his hands, he knew he loved her. And, in the process of allowing the hunter to heal her at all, she knew that she loved him back.

That sweet satyr girl does not mourn the scar over her heart; time is precious, and she is determined to not pre-mourn what has not yet died. Being a fairy creature the way she is, it is sometimes difficult to tell the difference between what has not yet happened with what is currently happening. It's also difficult to remember that, sometimes, arrows are invitations we didn't know we needed. The arrow ensures we closely inspect our hearts for wounds in need of healing. The arrow also reminds us to count our scars and be proud that we're yet living.

One day the faun will come to appreciate the scar over her heart; it will remind her of the day when the hunter's arrow flew true and yet she survived.

The satyr girl will, one day, find peace in the knowledge that not all arrows to the heart are fatal.

LOST ANGELES

If Earth was a goddess on the cover of a glossy magazine, she'd be the kind to insist that her cover not be Photoshopped because it's important for people to know what it looks like to age gracefully. Although, it wouldn't be quite fair because, even at four billion years old, Earth is a knockout. She's got the kind of age lines that let you know she's seen things like the extinction of an entire species and the rise of Sad Keanu as an internet meme. Sea is her twin sister, and they argue over who was born first—they each insist that she is four minutes older than the other. That argument's been going on for so long that it's been mostly forgotten, and all that's left in its wake are the remnants of an uneasy accord between the two.

If the Earth and the Sea were these women, then the Underworld is their younger sister that they wish they could claim was only related by marriage instead of by blood. Underworld would wear black leather pants and steel-toed boots and wouldn't be afraid of stepping on a neck every now and then. Neither would Earth or Sea for that matter, except the difference is neither of them delights in telling you about the time they popped the carotid artery of a dudebro who was using the hashtag #NotAllMen to harass some female gamers online. It's not like Underworld intentionally made him bleed from the inside out; he really brought it on himself with his addiction to six-dollar burgers with bacon and guacamole and deep-fried jalapeños with chili cheese. "Sho ga nai," Underworld would say—not because she speaks Japanese, but because she heard it in an anime once—before she took the dudebro to Lost Angeles where she made him live the rest of his afterlife in The Valley as punishment for his terrible life choices.

That isn't how I ended up here exactly. I mean, I have made my fair share of terrible life choices, but when you're immortal it kinda comes with the territory. It seems like forever ago that I first came down to Lost Angeles, which, I guess, is because it was forever ago. Time is totally a thing for me. It moves differently for gods, moves differently for mortals. There are two constants in Lost Angeles:

people always die and there's always traffic since the freeways are clogged with incoming souls. So if the dudebro wants to check out the Egyptian death rites exhibit at the Getty, it's going to take him fifty-seven years to get there. But who's to say if it'll actually feel like fifty-seven years to him? One thing's for certain, though: there's no punishment greater than being stuck on the 5 going south.

Olvera Street was like bubblegum dynamite. This was where Hades and I met when I slipped into the underworld against my mother's wishes. The crunch of cinnamon and sugar paved the narrow alley between the street vendors and cafes, while bougainvillea and marigolds dripped everywhere else, heavy with magenta and thick as tangerine smog. Mictlantecuhtli, king of the Aztec underworld, danced to the ritual drums with ayoyote seed pods on his ankle bones. Along with his band of ritual dancers, the skeleton king kept rhythm with the constant thrum of soul traffic that rumbled by on Alameda Street while their headdresses, made of eagle feathers and pheasant plumage, mesmerized the spirits that gathered in the plaza. The smell of sweet egg bread and bundles of burning sage comingled with car exhaust and moonwalked together through the air. The smoke from the ofrendas was still visible against the twinkle lights, and the sugar skulls were bright with pink flamingo and aquamarine icing. My favorite part of the night was when Mictecacihuatl, queen to the dancing skeleton king, would remove her bottom jaw and vomit up the stars she had eaten during the day back into the sky above Union Station. But, as the festivities died away, and the newly dead began to wander from the place where the Aztec gods performed their nightly rituals, I noticed a fox corpse at the base of one of the ancient magnolia trees.

I was taken by the ruin that bloomed there: eyes rotted out of the skull, nose skin shrinking away from its open mouth, and maggots feasting away on what was left. Surrendering to the cycle, how death begets life: these were things I would never know as the daughter of Demeter, being immortal the way I am. It's always been important to my mother that I understand the beauty to be made in life, so she spent centuries training me in all kinds of art. She said I was the goddess of spring, so it was my duty to dig down deep into the earth and bring forth the beauty I saw there. Who knew digging trenches was an art form? I do. Because I had to dig them. And after I dug for weeks, months really, my mother said now that the earth knew my hands and my sweat, it was ready to receive spring, and now that my hands knew the earth, I'd always be grounded. So why don't I be a doll and go and fill the soil back where it belongs? Oh, and I'll never have to worry about the earth responding to my touch again. Digging for digging's sake, right? Ya know, I adore Oscar, really I do, but there's a part of me that wants to rip up that manifesto of his while he and my mother watch. Although, knowing him, he'd probably just laugh, twirl his purple crushed velvet cape and compliment how strong my arms looked while I ripped his words to shreds, and my mother would say, "Must be from all that digging."

My mother claims her only regret in life is my name. This is absurd. Not that she has a regret, but that, in a life as long as hers, the one regret she has is my name. Persephone literally means "to destroy," but my mother had intended it to mean abundance. But good intentions are like mortal body parts, or maybe lives—it's difficult for me to keep those straight, but, either way, both are easily lost. And mortals, being the fickle creatures they are, saw my careful digging for spring as the most happy and enthusiastic kind of destruction—like a cotton candy pink bunny with a bazooka. It's probably no surprise that I've always liked my name. I think it's kind of badass.

So, even though it disheartens my mother, I seek out those places where life and death grow in lustful devotion to one another which was why I was drawn to Lost Angeles in the first place. The first time I came to the underworld was for a boy, my own personal Pretty Teen Dreamboat. I know. It's hella cliché and heteronormative in a way I'm not entirely comfortable with, but when you have an adolescence that's centuries long, then you get to judge. The boy was mortal (obvs), and I used to visit him in a hidden meadow where he collected rosebuds and thyme, and then we'd sprawl out across a thick bed of mint and hold hands. If you're into abstinence porn, then we would've been your teen idols.

Pretty Teen Dreamboat told me he loved that place because of how it smelled. And me, thinking he'd love me for being partially responsible for making this place, told him about the time I turned my best friend into the mint we were luxuriating upon because she had never really been my best friend. She was always saying my hair was too dark, my skin was too fair, and my arms were too muscular to be considered girly. So, I turned her into the opposite of what she was, and mint seemed to be that thing.

Pretty Teen Dreamboat didn't think my story was nearly quite so charming.

He ran away from me, even though I warned him not too, and he was torn apart by wolves, which used to happen way more often than it does now—at least I think so, it's difficult to keep all the timey-wimey bits straight since, especially in Lost Angeles, time moves differently in that I'm not entirely sure it exists at all. So I guess I knew that mortals died, ya know, intellectually, but it's not quite the same as seeing your very own Teen Dreamboat strewn across a hill. I asked my mother what would happen to him now, and she said he'd go to the Underworld, and that it was a terrible place, and that I was forbidden to visit. Which was pretty much all I needed.

Dying seems to really change a person. When I found this pretty boy I had not quite loved, but thought myself capable of loving, he was just wandering around the canals in Venice that divert parts of the Lost Angeles River Styx. You see, ours also doesn't have water in it, although we don't blame ours on droughts; our river is brimming with the spirits of the dead, and the canals were built to handle the overflow. And good ole Charon still runs the ferry back and forth, up and down the river (it's faster than the 101, trust).

So, even though I delighted mightily at defying my mother's wishes by being in Lost Angeles at all, I still felt a pang of guilt in my chest that I was there, that I managed to stumble upon the billboard perfect combination of life and death as embodied by, well, the body of the fox. Seasons exist on time, and since time is jacked here, the least I could do would be to use my power to bring just the tiniest bit of spring to this world.

There was life under the fox's body, just beneath the surface of the ground, with shoots aching to know more of the earth that was soft with spring. Bare earth, or dirt at all, is so rare in the concrete plains of Lost Angeles that it's hard to even find the ground, let alone be, like, grounded. So it seemed lucky that there was some ground at all for life to sprout under.

I knelt before the fox in all its aftermath, decomposing at the base of the gnarled roots of the magnolia tree, and I reached out my hand to inspire a single narcissus to unfurl from the ribcage. My power has always been in making (also digging), and I took pride in my handiwork: the petals, white as calaveras, framed an egg-yolk-yellow center.

My skin rolled over in gooseflesh right before I heard his voice.

"I've always found beauty in the moment of surrender," Hades said.

I have always been able to sense when Hades was near; his presence made me feel whole, the way I imagine the night sky feels when the moon comes out— never touching the moon, but happy to just be near him.

"You referring to the fox?" I asked as I stood to face him. Something ran wild in my chest at the sight of him. I was unnerved by the sharp ferocity of my desire to kiss him. I couldn't help but think of the spirit jaguars that roamed between here and Figueroa Street, gorging on the bodies of wandering souls in between the glass skyscrapers and the shadows they cast. I thought of the jaguar's hunger, and I envied his ability to sate it.

"What else?" Hades asked.

I looked out over the plaza at the cut paper banners in the shapes of skeletons, virgin mothers, and sacred hearts. Hundreds of candles lined the walkways and there was still the hint of chilies and chocolate in the air. "Growth is a form of surrender, too. Didja know that, at the Villa, there's a tree that's grown itself around a statue of my mother?"

"I assume I'll have to get a forty ready to pour at the hole it left in the ground after your mother had it removed," Hades said.

"No, actually. It's still there," I said.

"Like, whoa."

"She's always trying to force to me to see beauty in life up above—it's her way of trying to convince me that I don't need to come down here. Anyway, the tree trunk just, I don't know, encountered an obstacle and allowed itself to bend around what was in its way. It wasn't a surrender that came all at once, but a gradual release over time. When she noticed, I asked her to leave it. I told her that was it. That was the thing she keeps trying to make me see. And life was doing it."

"And what thing was that?"

"Surrender. Duh," I said, and I smiled wide at him.

"She'd be happy to see a sequoia surrounding my statues, but to allow it happen to an edifice of herself?" Hades matched my grin with a gameshow smile of his own and quirked his eyebrows in skepticism.

"Well, no one builds statues of you," I reminded him. "And, besides, it's true."

"I suppose growth is possible for even gods," Hades reached out his hand and I hesitated slightly before taking his in mine, making sure my gloves were on before we touched. When I was in Lost Angeles, no matter how much I ached to know the taste of a chimichanga with salsa verde, no matter how frosty the mango lassi, I did not eat or drink while in the underworld. The same rule applied to touching Hades: we weren't sure that if we touched, I'd be able to leave. It wasn't like Hades had a line of girlfriends before I showed up, so I took great pains to wear leather jackets and dresses that trailed the ground when I was with him; it wasn't as though I minded looking like a celestial version of Joan Jett.

On my first trip to Lost Angeles, I had wandered over to Little Tokyo, when Izanami, the Japanese death goddess, made me a bet. I'm kind of competitive, and she was like a volcano she was so enchantingly beautiful: it was difficult to look directly at her without feeling like my skin would melt off. She wore a kimono white as snow—now, being a goddess of the Greek persuasion, I'm not entirely familiar with snow itself, but the way I understand it, her kimono was white as the freshly fallen kind. And it was spotless; this is something I noticed because I'm the kind who can't wear white without spilling something on it. There was an elaborately tied blood red obi around her waist, and her hair was so black it had a violet sheen to it under the yellow street lights. She had painted just the middle of her lips the same shade of red as her belt, and it was difficult for me to remember the pretty boy who had been torn apart by wolves for whom I had wandered down here for in the first place.

I asked her what would we be wagering? She said a kiss was all she wanted. I admit, the terms of this bet didn't bother me at all. It's only just now that I realize she never asked me what I wanted. Probably because she knew I wanted the same thing.

Izanami bet me that she could find ice cream I could hold in my hand that wouldn't melt. I laughed because I love ice cream, and obviously I was going to win. But she reached out her hand and placed in mine the most perfect pastel green sphere in my hand. She said it was mochi ice cream. It was cold to the touch and I asked how it was possible. She said she'd tell me after I had a bite and she had her kiss.

And that's how I met Hades.

I admit, I'm not thrilled that we met under damsel-in-distress circumstances. I'm a god, I can take care of myself. But, also, sometimes, we all need rescuing from really, really pretty Japanese vampire death goddesses.

Hades was cool, man, like the sand the ocean kisses and then leaves behind when it's time for the tide to punch out. He was blue like the moon, and he had nebulas swirling in his eyes, and all I wanted was to be the night sky and wrap myself around him. He took me to a dive run by Pan—they were legion, so, at any one time there could be like twelve Pans in the joint—but the venue was run by the original god that accidentally invented panic by waking up a flock of sheep (but wanted to be known now for his neomodernistic approach to the flute). My favorite Pan though, was, is, and always will be: Freddie Mercury. Although, you haven't lived until you've heard Alip Ba Ta, one of the greatest Indonesian acoustic guitar players, finger pick "Bohemian Rhapsody" on a guitar while Freddie Mercury is brought to tears from the performance.

Freddie reckoned himself a musical slut after he found out calling himself a "musical prostitute" was as gauche as a rock star tying his own shoelaces. If another Pan tried to shame him, though, he'd say, "You say 'slut' like it's a bad thing," and then he'd stroll off harmonizing in that four-octave vocal range. Freddie Mercury: human soul equivalent of a mic drop.

Every Pan was different, but they all shared a similar ability to enchant their audiences through music. Like literally enchant, though. Hades told me if you weren't careful, you could walk outta that place hypnotized, and you *know* a Pan is going to take advantage of *that* situation. I mean, it's not a secret that I'm prone to enchantment.

That night, though, we talked about art. Hades told me Van Gogh sometimes stands in front of his *Irises, 1889* at the Getty and cries silent tears to himself; I did not tell him about digging in the dirt. We talked about love and how I always managed to feel empty around my Pretty Teen Dreamboat; we talked about how he had never fallen in love, and wasn't sure he wanted to stumble into it just to experience the sensation of falling—he said our people have a serious problem with falling into stuff (sleep, love, truth) and he wasn't interested in being another falling god when he had shit to take care of. We talked about how art and love collided when mortals befriended their mortality—I said I wish I could understand how to embrace such a thing I could never know; he said that maybe I should visit Lost Angeles more often and maybe, together, we'd both learn.

I was smitten, of course. Maybe it was the black leather, maybe it was his blue moon skin, maybe it was his '57 Chevy Bel Air with wing tips and a galactic paint job. But I was hooked, lined, and sinkered.

When I took his hand, he spun me in a circle beneath the twinkling lights of the ofrendas, the sodium bulbs of the streetlamps, and the moon. "Growth is just the half of things, you know. Life has no meaning without death."

"Kinda like how I have no meaning without you?" I teased in a singsong voice. Although, if I'm honest, it wasn't really a joke at all. I took the opportunity to spin myself into the crook of his arm, and I wrapped my arms around him, his body cool as the dark water ocean through his black shirt.

Hades fell silent a moment, and he pulled away from me to lean against the gazebo that encircled the magnolia tree. "I've plead our case to Zeus," he finally said as he cast his eyes downward.

I hopped up on the rail and gently bumped my shoulder to his, "I can handle my mother."

"You know how she is," Hades said.

"I do." I don't know what I bristled at more: the fact that I had to fight a battle at all or that I was in love with a god who did not think I could fight my own.

"Then you know," Hades said.

"I know you two have a lot in common."

"Oh really?" He laughed. "How's that?"

"Neither of you takes me seriously."

His expression flickered—almost imperceptibly—and I regretted saying it. However, I'd be lying if I said there wasn't a slight satisfaction in knowing that I could hurt him. That, having hurt him, I knew he loved me.

"Is that a switchblade in your mouth or are you just happy to see me?" Hades said.

"How can you love me when you obviously think me so weak?"

"This'll be good. Tell me, when was this so obvious?"

"When you went to Zeus."

"You know that's not what I meant," Hades said, and he fell silent a moment in that broody moon way of his. We were surrounded by paper bag luminaria and the scent of frankincense was heavy on the air, wards both against negative energy. I closed my eyes and braced myself against what Hades was about to say.

"What is this about really?" Hades asked, "Are you in love with me at all? Or are you just in love with this place, in love with the idea that being queen here is going to make up for the fact that you chose a life in the underworld? Are you just in love with the idea of making your mother happy?" His eyes, black as midnight during a new moon, looked into mine, and I could tell that he would steal my immortality if he could, if only to prove that he had been right all along: both his affections and my divinity had been misplaced.

I didn't think Hades had a right to be upset, for he knew how I felt about him, how I have always felt. I never understood why no one in the mortal realm built temples to Hades, why no one sang hymns in his name. If there was a moon god, he'd be mine, and I'd go on a wild hunt just to bring him back a Johnny Cash song, on virgin vinyl, as my sacrifice. He never fought Zeus or Poseidon for more than his share of the world; and, while Zeus got the earth and Poseidon got the sea, Hades was dealt the underworld, and though he wouldn't have chosen it for himself, he accepted the duty of keeping the souls of mortals safe with a Sinatran kind of grace. And he managed to keep peace among the polytheistic landscape of death gods in Lost Angeles to boot. Never seduced by the temptation of wreckage, he did not rape mortals, nor had he ever downed a single ship. He gave mortals, robbed of life and dignity by Zeus and Poseidon, dignity in death. Hades was just and fair, but everyone feared him because he was a chthonian god, the king of Lost Angeles and the underworld, where Death and Sleep play dice games just to pass the time.

This was the moment. I tried to kiss him for the first time in our centuries long waltz. I regretted that our first kiss would be in apology, but I tried nonetheless.

He pushed me away. "Don't," he said, his voice, not a warning, but an appeal to logic. "Be sensible."

My voice trembled, "How can you love someone you've never kissed?"

He turned away from me then, staring at the incandescent glow and flow of soul traffic on Alameda Street.

"I want you to have what I never did," he said and he turned back to look at me, "I want you to have a choice."

Thunder cracked straight through to my soul and I kissed him. It was not a polite kiss; it was fierce and sinewy and had razors along the edge. I didn't care about the consequences. I didn't want to leave, had never wanted to leave. Every time I did, a piece of my soul broke off and stayed with him. I was certain that eventually someone would find the scattered pieces of my soul strewn across the great sprawl of Lost Angeles, binding me here, to him, for good, and I knew when that day would come I would be glad. Relieved, even.

I pulled his hair and steered his lips to mine, and just as I felt our souls meet on our breath, he pushed me away again. He refused to let his eyes find mine, but it was too late. We were already connected, the one to the other, him and I, as we had always been.

The anima of what we created between our lips made the air around us thick, and I could feel the energy shift and swirl around us in a vortex, pushing us toward each other. The roses on the ofrendas lost their grip on the petals, and the rosehips took to the air, flickering ruby red and saffron yellow. I reached out my hands and gripped either side of his face and forced him to look at me.

"It doesn't feel true," he said as he covered my hands with his and gently brought my hands down, but he did not let go, our fingertips still entwined.

"What can I do?" I asked.

Hades did not reply.

"You can't expect me to be sane or sensible anymore. Every time I leave, I go away with pieces of myself missing, and pieces of you nestled in their place. I can't go on living away from you because these breaks are death. When I am with you, I am alive, and I would rather live with you in the city of the dead than walk around in the sunlight dead inside because you're not with me. I can no longer tolerate the obedience my mother has trained me to follow. But I do thank her for one thing. She raised me to have a voracious appetite, although, try as she might, she couldn't control what I craved. And what I crave is you. Not your flesh, although, yes, that, too, but I have a complete, devouring hunger for you. Hades, I only thought I loved you before; it was nothing like the certainty I harbor now. Have these centuries been so wonderful because our interludes were brief and stolen? Is it madness to believe this fierce kind of love can continue? It is a disgrace to continue to do nothing, to keep our options open, to be sensible. You might say this is a wild dream, but this is a dream I want to realize, and yes, I am wild. I am a goddess when I am with you, and I am almost terrified by it."

"You're too good at that," Hades said, and he walked over to me.

"At what?"

"Words. In general," he ran his talons through my hair. "You're too skilled for your own good. It can come across as disingenuous."

My voice cracked as I spoke, "How can the sky survive after knowing the closeness of the moon?"

For all my artful rhetoric, Hades kissed me, and I took his hand and led him to the base of the tree, where the fox had lost its dice game to Death. As we kissed, I guided his fingers to the curve of my hips, my hand over his, and he parted my thighs. I made love to him the way the fox had loved the flower that sprang forth in its chest. He kissed me the way jaguars tear into a kill. I wanted him to show me what it was to unmake the world, so that we could then remake it together. I wanted to lick the flesh from his bones, so that I may be made better for having known what it was like to have devoured a god. He showed me what it was to experience a million tiny deaths, and breaths, and sighs. I showed him that I understood that we were more than two parts of the same cycle, we were the union of the singular process that is life.

"I have a confession," Hades said into my hair as I rested my head on his chest.

"On a scale of one to Aries, how much do I want I hear this confession of yours?"

"Sometimes, when you're asleep, I watch you."

"Uh. Ew?"

"That's not the worst part," Hades said, laughing. "And, I'm not proud of it, but I have crept to the side of your bed, and breathed in the air as you slept so that we might share the same breath."

"That's gross."

"Which part?"

"The part where you're a creepy stalker," I said and when I sat up, I punched Hades playfully in the shoulder. "But, no, seriously. That's, like, mega creepy."

"I'm a death god, darlin'," Hades said, gently mocking me, "Creep comes with the territory."

"It's a good thing you're a king," I said.

Hades pulled away to look at me with exaggerated horror, "What?"

"Kidding!" I said. I lifted his hand to my face and buried my cheek in his palm, "What do we do now? I've got a taste for infinity now. I kind of don't want to give it up."

"I've got an idea," Hades said and he pointed to the narcissus growing in the fox's ribcage. "Give me your flower, and it'll be done."

"I hate to break it to you, but I think we already played that game," I said.

"The flower, and the fact that you made it, is the key," he said, ignoring my tailor made innuendo. "Give it to me, and you'll be my wife and queen. It's a union that neither your mother, nor Zeus himself can break."

Not even gods can kidnap the willing.

INK CAN TAKE MANY FORMS
IF YOU ALLOW IT

Once upon a time, there was a piece of paper. It was fine and made of linen, and its only dream was to be filled with ink. Since the paper was pulpy and soft, it knew the pen that would write a story upon its page would leave more than just ink behind. It would leave an indelible mark as well as an ineradicable stain, and the page was glad to believe that one day it would know what it was to hold a story inside its mind-belly the way only paper can—since every page is a text, every page is a body unto itself.

When the page finally met a pen, it was a fountain pen made of green marble and brass finishings. It had a tortoiseshell case and its very own well of the blackest ink money could buy. This particular ink, the fountain pen told the page, was made of shadows scavenged from the walls of buildings in Hiroshima. The page, not knowing much of the world, thought that this kind of ink sounded very fine indeed, and, so when the fountain pen invited the page to make itself very flat—the better to write upon, my dear—the page did so willingly.

"You have to be flatter than that," the fountain pen said to the page.

So the piece of paper stretched itself as low to the writing surface as it thought it could go.

"You have to think flatter thoughts than that," the fountain pen said.

"Flatter than what?" the page asked, quite perplexed as it was sure one side was completely in touch with the surface.

"Think flat as a vinyl forty-five of Nancy Sinatra singing slightly off-key—wait! No! Think flatter than Nancy even!" the fountain pen urged.

So, making itself as flat as, and as wide as, what a piece of paper understood Nancy Sinatra to be like, the page stretched itself as flat as it could possibly go.

"Perfect," the fountain pen said.

And the page was glad to make the fountain pen so proud.

But just as the piece of paper expected to know what the brass filament of the fountain pen would feel like upon its linen leaf, a pair of silver scissors cut the page into a thousand tiny pieces.

And the page never saw the fountain pen again.

The paper's heart was broken, or more accurately, cut. Now, it would surely never know what it was like to be filled with ink. It could never contain a complete story of its own—which had been the paper's one and only dream. The shorn page would only ever know fragments of a larger narrative, bits and phrases. Words like bone and smoke and water—words small enough to fit on tiny cuts of paper, but, perhaps, when artfully arranged would create a cohesive whole, even if the page would never know all the story at once, even if the page would never know what it was like to hold beautifully wrought prose in its mind-belly.

One day, the paper, and all its disparate parts and strips, met a needle. The needle was very small indeed, but it was sharp and true and saw all the tiny pieces of the page as a beautifully wrought work of art all on its own. It asked the page and its many pieces for permission to sew the paper back together again.

The page had never thought its pieces could be joined again. The page had thought that once the scissors made its cuts, that was the end of the page. But it hadn't been the end. The page had survived. A couple of its pieces might have floated away in the meantime—but that was to be expected after being made into cut paper.

So, the page gave the needle permission to sew as it saw fit. The page figured what was the worst that would happen? It had already been cut to pieces.

The needle brought out its very own spool of thread. It was red, like roses and rubies and every other proper 'r' word in the *Oxford English Dictionary*, and the needle carefully arranged the pieces of the paper into a mosaic, and then the needle artfully sewed the pieces together with neat zigzag stitching.

After the work was finished, the page felt full for the first time, like it contained a story of its own in its mind-belly the way only pieces of paper could. "How beautifully sewn I am!" The page said to the needle, "I'm not a rectangular piece of paper anymore! You've made me full and round!"

If a needle with a length of thread still clinging in its eye could blush, then this one surely would have.

"I embroidered something in the seams," the needle said, "I hope you don't mind."

The page could feel the story deep down in its newly fashioned seams, and it read: *In your seams, my infinite dreams.*

It wasn't the ink the page had been looking for. But the needle and thread were exactly what the page, and all its magnificent pieces, needed.

From time to time, the page and the needle take apart the red thread seams and reassemble the paper's parts in whatever order or shape they can dream up. Sometimes the pieces of the page are arranged into a castle tower, sometimes a pirate ship. But the pieces are always beautifully sewn with red thread.

And the page and the needle lived happily ever after, sewing up stories along the way.

5X5

Dear Scully,

I should've been suspicious of the girl in the lab coat offering me psychic ice cream. But with you and your ponytail, the psychic ice cream just seemed so harmless. After it gave me a brain freeze that'd make the Sierra Nevada mountains jealous, imagine my surprise when I started hearing people's thoughts—thank science it's only temporary! Good call on that, by the way—being able to permanently hear kids snarking to themselves about how you suckered me into testing your experiment for you is not exactly what I would call "an acceptable side effect."

You were too polite to ask out loud today, but, yes, there is a reason I'm arriving during the final week of camp. I'm only here because I won a scholarship after winning my school's science fair. In a school of forty-two students, it's not exactly difficult to come in first. After I filled out the registration, though, some guy called to make sure I had correctly filled out the forms. He said most people use the scholarship to defer the cost of the other seven weeks. "Like a discount!" he told me. He sounded really perky, like he'd make a commission off my enrollment or something.

Even with a discount, my family can't afford to send me here the whole eight weeks. So, I decided to come this final week to participate in the science fair since first prize gets a college scholarship. Because, where I'm from, we don't dream about going to college. Around here, we grow up hoping to just get a spot in the military or to find a plot of tillable soil for a pot farm.

But after having seen the experiments y'all have been working on for seven weeks straight—there's you with the psychic ice cream; the dude with the temporally displaced printer that "prints" first issues of *Detective Comics #27*—how is that a science experiment? It's more performance art, right? He's "printing" as many copies of *Detective Comics #27* as he can, all of which technically qualify as authentic as the original, in an effort to devalue the actual original issue. This is an economics experiment, a performance arts piece maybe, but not a science experiment. (And what does he have against Batman??)

Anyway, between you and that dude, plus seeing how everyone is so tight with each other, I started to wonder why did I come at all? What did I think I was going to be able accomplish in seven days?

I am so far behind.

So, even though the other kids are probably right. I was "too country" to know better than to taste your ice cream, I don't regret it for a second. Because when you raised your eyebrows at me, nodded your head slightly in the direction of that dude, and thought, very clearly, *I hate that guy*, I knew we were meant to be friends.

By the way, what does 5x5 mean?

X,
Fox

P.S. Yes, it's my real name. I heard you wonder about it earlier today, too.
P.P.S. (Is P.P.S. a thing? Maybe I just made it up. Whatevs. What's the deal with the case of luciferase enzyme in the back room?)

Sugarloaf Fine Sciences Summer Camp
Bunk Note Reply: Cabin Lovelace
07.13

Fox,

1. Why do you keep calling me Scully?
2. What was your experiment that won your school's science fair?
3. I really do hate that guy. Yes, I agree: his experiment is not really a scientific one; especially considering the science he is employing in service to his thought experiment is not necessarily cutting edge, but,

instead, is the kind of retro throwback that tends to win over nostalgic adults. (But I honestly don't know what he has against Batman. I suspect someone in his family read their copy of *Detective Comics #27* when it was meant to be an heirloom, thus decreasing its value by taking it from "Mint Condition" to merely "Near Mint.")

4. I'm glad you decided to come to Sugarloaf. It's been hard for me to make friends here because it's generally hard for me to make friends anywhere; but, also here, people kept stealing my ice cream to find out who likes each other.

5. The etymology of 5x5: you might be familiar with it as I originally learned it (through colloquial and pop cultural uses). I promise once you know the meaning, you'll start noticing it everywhere. But 5x5 actually comes from old radio codes for broadcasting, which include a standard transmission check. Volume on a scale of 1-5; clarity on a scale of 1-5. So, 5x5 is shorthand for "loud and clear," which is sometimes also used and has been incorporated as slang. I find it appropriate shorthand for the purposes of my experiment, since I am trying to ascertain the volume and clarity of the psychic ice cream.

6. As for the luciferase enzyme: I don't know. The girl who ordered it special the first week of camp went home sick before it even arrived. Are you thinking of using it for your experiment somehow?

—Scully (I guess)

Sugarloaf Fine Sciences Summer Camp
Bunk Note: Cabin Lamarr
07.14

Scully,

My experiment studied the effect of synthetic bioluminescence on plant growth. I hypothesized that if plants could absorb light during the day and convert it to food, then they could be bioengineered to produce the same luciferase enzyme found in fireflies—even though I've never actually seen a firefly since they're not native to California. But my plants had a very long persistence of phosphorescence when energized by normal sunlight as opposed to relying on a chemical reaction. My goal was to create marijuana that could continue to grow at night by reflecting off each other, lowering reliance on artificial grow lights.

Yeah, I come from a family of pot farmers. Sure, it seems glamorous on *Dawson's Field*, but most of the time my family makes ends meet by scrapping metal at the end of the month to keep the lease on our land. When there's water enough for the land even, that is. I really should've been trying to find an alternate way to manufacture water, right? You know what plants in California don't need? More sun when there's barely any water.

I'm sorry people were stealing your project. I think they're just fascinated by the possibility of hearing the truth of things. But, maybe also scared too—because seriously, what experiment is going to possibly compete with psychic ice cream on Saturday? (Not temporally displaced 3D printers, I assure you—that technology is so ten years ago.)

When we were in lab, I "heard" a bunch of the seniors are heading up to the roof of the lab after lights out. So, if you sneak out of the cabin with me tonight, I will totally show you the altar I've built to my moon goddess, Dana Scully. (The altar is made of *The X-Files*.) So you'll finally understand why I was so excited to have found my very own Scully.

Plus, you both have red hair.

5x5: yes, I am totally thinking about using that luciferase somehow. Just don't know how yet. Kinda hate the project I won my science fair with. So yeah. I figure I'll come up with an idea… any day now.

X,
Fox

Fox,

1. I'm not really into spooning with strangers, but last night was fun. Not that you're a stranger; not exactly anymore anyway. But the others pretty much are. I didn't even ask the guy whose tablet we borrowed to stream *X-Files* his name, and it didn't seem to occur to anyone that it was rude

not to ask. There was a specific kind of freedom in it all that I'm not used to, and not sure I'm entirely comfortable with, but then I'm uncomfortable most of the time anyway.

2. As a fellow Californian, I, too, have never seen fireflies. I've always wanted to, though.

3. I've never seen *Dawson's Field*. I'm not really into series reboots. But I assure you: farming doesn't seem like my idea of glamour. But I'm from L.A.

4. Yeah, you should totally come up with an alternate method to manu facture water. Why haven't you done this already? </end sarcasm> And don't be so hard on your school science fair experiment: it got you here. Plus, it sounds legitimately interesting.

5. You've only got three more days before the fair. So. You know. No pressure. I'm totally lying: you need to come up with something! If you need help coming up with ideas, I'm here.

—(happy to be compared to) Scully

Sugarloaf Fine Sciences Summer Camp
Bunk Note Reply: Cabin Lamarr
07.15-02

Scully,

Yeah, the rolling brownouts up here last year had everyone tripping on ways to grow their plants with constant light. So I was kinda proud of my experiment at the time. It only halfway worked, though. I got the plants to glow in the dark, and that's pretty much it. I had no access to a genome compiler or the proper cultures of bacteria to properly replace the chemical reactions.

See, it's not hard to come in first when the next coolest experiment was a kid with a baking soda volcano.

But I honestly have no idea what I'm doing for Saturday. There isn't really time to do anything competitive. Mostly, I'm just happy to help you with yours because I am absolutely in awe of your brain, and you should win all the things.

Question: are the brain freezes completely necessary? They seem necessary, especially because of the way you smile to yourself in lab after you say "Sorry!" to me during one of the brain freezes—even though you are clearly not sorry at all! And you shouldn't be. You can't help it if you're a badass scientist. You invented psychic ice cream, for chrissakes.

There was a feeling on the roof last night that I've never felt before, too. And I wasn't going to say anything because I was certain it was going to seem too country or you'd chalk it up to lingering effects of the ice cream; but, last night was the safest I have ever felt—and this was in the arms of girls and guys I didn't even know. I just enjoyed cuddling without having to worry about where it was all going.

I confess, when I woke up this morning, I felt an ache in my heart when you weren't there, or anyone else for that matter, because we were all back in our own bunks instead of on our backs absorbing residual heat that was baked into the roof earlier in the day. I enjoyed the closeness with you all on the roof while I stared up at an uninterrupted sky. It's the kind of closeness I've been looking for my entire life—the ease with which we just rested our heads on each other's shoulders and streamed *The X-Files*—I want more of that in my life, even though it's going to disappear soon.

X,
Fox

Sugarloaf Fine Sciences Summer Camp
Bunk Note Reply: Cabin Lovelace
07.15-03

Fox,

1.   The ice cream has to be super-cooled in order for the temporary telepathic effects to last as long as possible—the restriction of the blood flow effects the absorption rate. So the brain freeze is part of the reason why it works. I also want the effects to be temporary—since you've already experienced some of the reasons why.

2.   Even while it is happening, I know the friendships we are developing on the roof at night aren't sustainable outside of that space—not even sustainable in the lab the next day, as you so heartlessly pointed out after this afternoon's test. (I really do hate that guy!) And, usually, I would resist giving myself over so completely to a candle I can clearly see is

about to burn out. But, instead, with the science fair only three days away, my eyes are open wide enough to memorize everything I can, as deeply as I can, so I can carry you all (mostly you) with me even after we leave.

3. Thank you kindly (in regards to your thoughts about my brain and things). But I don't want you to feel obligated to help me. Helping me is not a price you must pay in order to have my friendship. Also: if you think my brain is so brilliant, remember my brain will help yours pull off whatever you need in time for Saturday. I don't want you to feel like there's no time to do something amazing. We're good at sneaking out after hours, after all.

4. Where do you disappear to during lunch? You're always around for breakfast and dinner—I know because one of us always manages to receive inter-camp mail, but I have no idea where you go at lunch time. Are you working through lunch at the lab?

—S

Scully,

Will you help me develop a serum that will infuse me with the qualities of an anglerfish? If you do, I would take that vial of purple goo right here, right now, right this very moment. And I would drink it down gladly in hopes that I would grow gills and filament and be able to find a home, beside you, deep beneath the ocean's surface—where the crushing force of the water would surely crush any other creature, save for the two of us, who were built to withstand the high pressure environment, but also uniquely built to amuse each other. And I would make my bioluminescent filament dance in hopes that it might attract your attention, just once. Because once is all I would need—since we would be the last two anglerfish in this deep end of the dark sea.

X,
Fox

Fox,

1. That's really, very sweet, but you realize that all anglerfish, as you know them, are female anglerfish—as the species has evolved one of the most extreme forms of sexual dimorphism in the animal kingdom: in which the males, literally the size of minnows, fuse with the females to form a parasitic union in which he becomes little more than an appendage that produces occasional sperm?
2. I am not interested in any such union. I am only 16.

—S

Dear Scully,

If you were a firefly and I was a wolf, I would be glad to chase you all through the summer night, not caring where we ended. Being a wolf, I'd be clever enough to leave tracks behind to follow on the mountain path so that I might find my way back home again at the end of our adventure—at which point you would take to chitinous wings and spark a glow that would make even barred and spiral galaxies jealous.

But I am melting into the darkness with my black wolf coat, and it's difficult to tell where the shadows end and I begin. It's becoming difficult to remember which way is home because our adventure has shown me wonders that I always thought best left for other creatures to pursue.

Until you showed me, I am not sure I had ever rightly examined a firefly and appreciated its secret for flying. Until you gave me a spoon, I had never tasted ice cream. Until you sang, I never heard music. These things existed before, of course, but I never knew enough to know how to appreciate them. But they now contain the secrets of the universe and contain a kaleidoscopic kind of beauty that my black wolf heart can barely take the colors.

So here I am, quite desperately, in my own wolfish way, trying to find my way back home. But my wolf legs and my wolf heart are crying out to run, and each wants nothing more than to run to you.

And so, Scully, this is where our story rests for now. We: as two different creatures as Difference could fathom in the deep, dark depths of her imagination.

And yet the experiment must go on, and so it will. But neither my wolf heart nor anglerfish soul can give up the chase that easily.

X,
Fox

Fox,

1. You are much better with emotions than I am—which is weirdly appropriate given our monikers. So, please, know that in the cases of both Agent Scully and myself, a lack of expression does not necessarily telegraph a lack of emotion. I have practiced the fine art of restraint for years in preparation for college applications. Utilizing this skill, I have mastered the violin, volunteer work, and Virginia Woolf. So remember: still waters and things.

2. I enjoy cuddling with you on the roof. And I greatly enjoy collaborating with you in lab. And I find myself reading and then re-reading your letters over and again throughout the day, and my breath catches in my chest when the inter-camp mail gets delivered at breakfast and dinner—you still haven't told me where you go at lunch. And while I respect and admire you—and I love your brain, too, don't forget—I am a scientist. I am not naturally predisposed to effusiveness the way you are.

3. But know that I think very highly of you. That I greatly esteem you. That I like you.

4. And that's right, I just totally *Sense and Sensibilitied* you because I'm a big

nerd. But I'm pretty sure that's why we get along so well.

—Scully

Scully,

Let me tell you what is natural.

The way your mind shines so bright that I am nearly blinded by your light—woman was never meant to stare directly into the sun.

The way you sing to yourself when you walk between cabins when you think no one is listening—or maybe the way you sing because you secretly want someone to hear you singing and admire from a distance.

The way your ponytail bounces as you walk.

The way I get to feel special because, in the midst of everyone working on their experiments—experiments they'll most likely forget about as soon as college application season is over—I discovered you.

X,
Fox

Fox,

1. Your psychic frustration with me yesterday—yes, I admit I "sampled my own product" while you weren't looking—makes me think you should be with someone as equally free in their expression as you. Because I don't think I will ever rightly be the kind of girl you want me to be. Freely expressing yourself is the quality I love most about you, but

it is not something that will ever feel natural to me. Sneaking out, and, generally, breaking rules is not something that feels natural to me, either, but I did these things to be with you. But, at a certain point, I have to accept what I can offer to you as myself without trying to change to suit you—also, I suspect, if I fundamentally changed myself to suit you anyway, I would lose one of the reasons you like me so well.

2. I know that this might be painful to read—but I like you too much to give you false hope the way I have seen both girls and boys do here to each other all summer long. My hope is that our friendship will be able to withstand not being at Sugarloaf, because you are a once in a lifetime kind of friend, and I would like to know you the rest of my life.

—Scully

Dearest Scully,

I may go on to do other things in either science or art, but last night will always remain my masterpiece.

I realized on the first day I arrived that my presence here was something of a joke. I could never really be in the running for the science fair here. Even if you all hadn't had a seven week head start on your projects, you had years of preparation before any of us ever stepped foot at Sugarloaf. And that's okay. I felt weirdly triumphant in this realization. I think it's okay to know when to give up. And I think it's okay to feel triumphant in that knowing.

When you look back on last night, promise me that you will remember that there were hundreds of them, thousands, really. Remember the way we held hands as we each held a bucketful of moonlight and seeded the woods around camp with the moth larvae I genetically modified to glow in the dark. I couldn't bring you fireflies—invasive species and all that—but remember the way the glow worms spread themselves amongst the limbs, and don't forget the way they dripped themselves down phosphorescent strands of silk and gently swayed in the night breeze.

But, most of all, remember that none of this would've been possible without you.

By the time we set the last of the glow worms loose, their bioluminescence was so bright that the camp started waking up and coming outside to investigate the phosphorescent glow. The trees were lit up with soft shades of minty neon green against a night sky, a shade of blue so deep it's only been seen by scientists in deep sea submersibles—maybe hunting anglerfish?

This week issued me a challenge: to either grow or diminish, and you gave me the power to grow. Even when I wanted to resist it, even when I was afraid of what growing would mean, even when I was afraid of where my anglerfish soul, my wolf heart, and the glow worms would take me. And I can't thank you enough for this gift.

I realize there's a part of you that will always think I need you to be different than you are. Don't. I realize there's a part of you that will always think I made a terrible decision in not submitting the glow worms to the science fair. It wasn't. It's important to me that you know I wouldn't have spent this week any other way, I wouldn't do anything differently even now, and that I regret nothing about turning my experiment into a love letter for you.

I would've made a truly terrible scientist. But I'm in love with a truly remarkable one.

XO,
Fox

Sugarloaf Fine Sciences Summer Camp
Bunk Note: Cabin Lovelace
07.19-02

F,

5x5

—S

THE FROG MAIDEN

You have so mastered the fine art of transformation that I like to imagine you a Frog Maiden, a steward queen of soft mud, deep waters, and sunken treasure. You fear not murky waters because you know what it is to dig your hands deep in the muddy bottom of still ponds and find pirate treasure there; you know what it is to navigate fallen trees in opaque water with your eyes closed.

I like to imagine you with strong frog legs, dearest—green with faint stripes of robin's egg blue, with a speckling of yellow freckles—and your feet are wide and webbed. You're immensely proud of how far these limbs have carried you and yours. And you've done it all by necessarily leaving the quiet, still pond behind, exchanging the cloudy, chocolate pond water for rivers people promised would be sparkling and clear.

But, you've spent so much time in rushing rivers lately that your sensitive, amphibious skin is aching, and there's an ache in your legs, too, and these aches echo in the chambers of your heart.

It's okay to leave the river, my lovely frog maiden—the current isn't for everyone. And deciding that the river isn't for you does not mean that you'll never want to swim in one again. Deciding that the river isn't for you does not mean that your strong frog legs have hidden a secret weakness all these years.

Deciding to leave the river simply means you tried river life and found that it wasn't for you—and even then, it doesn't mean the river won't be right for you forever, it just means the river is not right for you for now.

It's okay to fear going back to the pond, too, dearest. You've metamorphosed a lot since you've been away, traversing streams and rivers and oceans. Your skin is rougher than it used to be when all it knew was the safe murk of brown pond water. It's okay to be afraid that a part of you will always secretly crave the rush of the river.

You are one of the few people who truly understand that there are many different types of bodies of water. You would never expect Brother Catfish born in a muck pond to make his way in the sea. So, too, you must turn that kindness and understanding on yourself.

You must find the body of the water that you can call home now—not the body of water you think you ought to call home. Not the body of water you think you'll grow into five years from now. There's an ache in your legs and a sensitivity in your skin. Your body is asking you to listen closely. It has never failed you; this body has carried you thousands of miles. All your body wants is to serve your soul.

But now is the time to fill your lungs with breath, dearest. Now is the time to cradle that breath in your lungs until you crave truth as you crave air. Now is the time to sink down deep into the mud and see what desires you find hidden there.

My hope for you is that, regardless of which body of water you call home, you listen to the ache in your legs and skin. I hope you find mud and water in which you can sink down deep, and your heart will know peace. And once you've found that peace, you'll sink a hand into the muddy bank and allow yourself to pull out the secret sunken treasure that only your heart will recognize.

You are the queen of transformation and sunken treasure, after all.

IT'S OKAY TO LAY DOWN
THE MACHETE

You have worked hard in this life. So very hard. You were in a jungle with only a machete and you managed to carve your own path out of the canopy; that path has taken you clear across to the other side of the world.

This path was forged by your sweat and your stamina alone. And you got where you were hoping to go. Do you know how rare this is? This is a beautiful and rare moment in a life.

It is time to rest, dearest.

If I were with you right now, I would brush your hair and make you tea brewed for sleep, and I would hang fairy lights around the edge of your bed. Because only in the pitch dark do these thoughts come to us; so, even in our sleep, we need a little help keeping the darkness at bay. And I know you're not afraid of darkness: you, who spent years in the jungle, forging your own path alone. I imagine your arms are strong and sinewy, and you left enough banana leaves in your wake to build a city of finely crafted huts.

It is time to rest, dearest.

My hope for you is that it is a joyful rest. One in which you will sleep deep and breathe in the labors of your love. Because it was love that spurred you on through the jungle.

When you lost the map and had to navigate by memory alone, it was love that guided you. When your arms grew tired and your hands were blistered by the machete, it was love that hacked at the mangrove trees in your way. You may have questioned the turns you made along your path. You may look at your uncalloused hands now and yearn for the ache in your biceps that comes with hacking.

But it is time to rest, dearest.

You deserve the quiet contentment of a path well-forged. You deserve to be proud of those years in the jungle. They changed you. And this time of quiet restfulness will change you, too. Not in the ways you think it should. Not in the ways you may have expected—you, who spent years sucking the spit out of snake bites;

you, who spent years bartering for clean socks and dry boots; you, who spent years malnourished in the jungle.

Grow fat, dearest. Grow fat and sleepy, like a Buddha statue or a hobbit. Take pride in your belly. Pinch an inch and smile wide and then roll over and sleep some more. You've earned it.

And when you've finally had your fill of sleep, you will wake up one morning with a dream—a dream that stays with you even after you've had your rice and cereal. A dream that will start out small, sprouting in the dark. This dream will be worth the sleeping, dearest.

But first, you must rest.

MERMAID CAFÉ

∴FINDS∴ MERMAID CAFE ***

Mermaids are good luck, the menu says. The story goes that, when The
Captain grew too old and too weathered and too jaded by the sea, he docked his
ship and opened Mermaid Café right in the harbor, complete with cargo nets and
aquariums filled with neon fish, all of which too tropical for the likes of Dublin.
There's an oaken mermaid bust, arms outstretched above her head, reaching for
a distant shore that once guided The Captain's ship across the Irish Sea in murky
storms.

Customers take pleasure in the name and atmosphere as they enjoy the
mermaid paintings by Irish artists done in watercolors from Kilkenny, oils from
Thurles, and charcoal from Limerick. There's full-color mermaid photography
where voluptuous models are styled in turquoise fins, magenta clamshells, and
chartreuse flowing wigs. There are mermaids swimming through reeds, basking
on rocks, barely visible from beneath the surface of the water. But along the back
wall there's a rounded door nearly hidden by red velvet drapes and dark
wooden paneling. Near this door, arranged in a tidy row, are a series of plainly
framed black and white photos of mermaids swimming near gargantuan,
water-logged chests of pirate treasure; of mermaids floating in water, in which
the bubbles are nearly the size of their delicate bodies. These mermaids are less
human, more fish. The delicate hands are webbed, or perhaps it's a trick of the
flash. If the photos weren't in black and white, it's clear that these bodies would be
green, and maybe even deep-sea purple. The mouths are wide and the teeth are
tiny; lips are simply an afterthought.

In this little sea-docked café that sells both frothy vanilla lattes and Irish coffee, the menu features a delicacy in Gaelic: *Leannàn sì*. Not even the locals really

speak the language anymore; you have to go deep in the Tipperary for that. When asked, the waitresses simply say, "It's expensive." At four-hundred-seventy-five euro, the dish is, indeed, extravagantly priced. The Captain only enters the restaurant proper when a particularly curious, and particularly rich, customer orders *Leannàn sì* after having been seduced by the weight of the thick, padded leather menu in his hands. Then, ripe and old, The Captain, with his grizzled beard and gnarled knuckles, escorts the man behind the velvet drapes and rounded door to his own quarters, whereby the door is padlocked for privacy. Some customers enjoy the theatrics of The Captain. Others should be prepared to be startled by the drama, but then also be prepared to allow themselves to chuckle and apologize for whatever trepidations they felt.

Customers wait for four hours in The Captain's Quarters, where cameras and film spill across an executive's desk, coiling in the scant moonlight that filters in through the windblown glass. There are books to read, of course. A library encircles the room, encroaching upon the space making it even smaller. *The Odyssey, The Picture of Dorian Gray, Peter Pan* are all bound in Moroccan goatskin bindings and gilded with gold leaf.

When The Captain finally emerges, he holds a serving tray made of pure silver and simply lifts the lid. No flourish. No tomfoolery. No tricks of light or hand. But there, upon a delicate filigreed platter, lays a tiny, splayed mermaid: smaller than customers may imagine. The skin on the middle of her chest is peeled back with entomological pins to reveal her miniscule heart, fluttering so fast as to appear still—save for the pleasurable hum of the aorta and ventricles.

The mermaid tastes of licorice and uni, a not unpleasant combination.

DE DEABUS MINORIBUS EXTERIORIS THEOMAGICAE

De Daebus Minoribus Exerioris Theomagicae: Textual Criticism and Notes
on the Book as Object, A Bibliographic Study by
Donna Morgan, Ph.D. Candidate,
Department of English,
Miskatonic University

Reproduction of Title Page:

#

DE DEABUS MINORIBUS EXTERIORIS THEOMAGICAE:
A Difcourfe on the Invocations of
the Lesser Outer Goddesses;
Grounded in her Creator's Proto-
Chimiftry, and verifi'd by a practicall
Examination of Principles in the Greater Dimenfion.

By Septimia Prinn
The Voice of Idh-yaa:
She was a woman
with a tome.

Zoroafter in Oracul. (Zoroaster in Oracle.)

Audi Ignis Vocem. (Listen to the Fire)

(handwritten Elizabeth Breedlove)

LONDON,
Printed by E.B For H.Vondrak at the
Castle in Thorn-hill. 1650.

Binding:

1. 3"x5" in size.
2. Octavo binding (eight leaves per quire).
   a. Never seen an octavo so small; generally duodecimos are this size because of the folding of paper.
3. No evidence of rebinding; most likely not forgery; provenance unknown.
   a. Binding is intact but well-worn from frequent use.
   b. Cover in serviceable condition; leather is visibly weathered from repeated handling; dirty (oils from hands depositing in leather).
      b.i. Threads on back cover, where binding meets book structure, are raised; thick thread looks like "skeletal fingers" binding requires to cover.
      b.ii. Upon closer inspection, "skeletal fingers" are not just abnormally thick twine bindings; appear to be bound with articulated bones, with thread carefully sewn through the bone connecting binding to cover.
      b.iii. Judging from shape and lightness of bones, I suspect they are wings from a single bat; search on library databases suggest that this technique has not been seen before; email sent to Professor Dane to confirm.
         — A headache is forming with intense pressure behind eyes; artificial light in Special Collections is becoming painful.
4. Considering occult subject matter of text, small size, slim width: Binding suggests it was designed with secrecy in mind; could easily be concealed on body.
   a. I postulate this was a practicing occultist's grimoire.

Paper:

1. This octavo is printed exclusively on vellum, still pungent.
   a. Vellum most likely made of pigskin, although this does not have the same color or scent as the vellum commonly sourced in London during this era; perhaps chemically treated to achieve a whiter transparency, hence the remnant smell; possibly sheepskin.
2. On page 50, quire E, on the 7th leaf, on the face of one of the only decorative plates in the book, an illustration, beneath which these hand written words appear (Translations are my own):

Idh-yaa Lythalia Vhuzompha
Shub-Niggurath Yaghni Yidhra (names of lesser outer goddesses)
Dare licentiam ad ut eam in servitium vestrum arma capere milites, (Give her permission to arm soldiers in your service.)
Septimia Prinn (proper name of author)
Deas à Conciliis, & Oracul Indiciarius, (Goddess' Council & Indicarius (?) of the Oracle)
DoȜtor Utriusque Naturam & Diᵥinam. (Doctor of Both Natural Laws & Divine)

3. At this site, a discoloration on the page. A watermark, perhaps; appears to be lettering.
   a. Not aware of watermarks in this period using words instead of symbols.
   b. Asked for a cold (fiber optic) light, but Carlo, the Special Collections librarian, claims they do not have one.
      b.i. Certain I used one in Special Collections earlier this week.
   c. Carlo provides me with table lamp.
      c.i. Why is Carlo keeping the cold light from me?
4. Place watermarked leaf over table light, but nothing lights up beneath, meaning it is embossed.
   a. Hold book at eye level, single leaf against overhead lights, read aloud: "*Eram quod es; eris quod sum.*" (I was what you are; you will be what I am.)
5. The book features deckled edges and is adorned with heavy speckling, most likely quill ink; the speckles are a brown, sepia tone.
   a. Quill ink generally made with iron in this era, which oxidizes over time; same color of oxidization is on edges, as well as the handwritten portions of the text.
   b. As Special Collections closed for the day, I placed tome on dissertation cart.
      b.i. Somehow tome ended up in my bag.
      b.ii. Will continue textual analysis at home; will return text to cart tomorrow.
6. The vellum is desiccated, making the edges of each page razor sharp.
   a. Slit tip of thumb as I turned a page.
      a.i. Kind of cut that's so deep it doesn't bleed right away and looks as though the skin never separated.

    b. Turned page, left bloody thumbprint.

        b.i. Went to get cotton swab and peroxide to lift stain out.

            — Blood is gone.

Illustration/Decoration:

1. Title page: encased in border depicting moon phases.

    a. Phases of moon include black circles that transition from black crescents into black, outlined crescents, representing shifting of new moon to full moon.

    b. Out of the corner of my eye, while I typed those observations on my laptop, the moons appeared to be actively shifting, as if animated.

        b.i. Possible that arrangement of the moon gradations are an optical illusion.

2. Page 51: single full-page woodcut featuring sextet of lesser outer goddesses.

    a. Above woodcut reads: *Supplication of the Unfathomable Ones,* beneath which the woodcut is printed.

        a.i. When I looked at this page to double-check the heading, the printed text was no longer in English, but what I can only presume is a cuneiform of Latin and Sumerian.

    b. Woodcut features worm-like Idh-yaa; sylvan Lythalia; Vhuzompha covered in multiple sets of eyes, mouths, as well as male and female genitalia; horned goat goddess Shub-Niggurath suckling infant devil at breast; many-tentacled Yaghni; and beautiful dream-witch Yidhra.

    c. Under woodcut, the following is handwritten: *Ungerent hoc in meo sanguine.* (Anoint this text in my blood.)

        c.i. Whenever I look at the book, the pages flicker and flash, like the popping lights of a camera.

            — I do not remember falling asleep, but I must have passed out from the headache because the next thing I know, I was lifting my head from my desk and it was after midnight. I'm so close to being done analyzing this book, I'm just going to power through.

3. Portrait of Septimia Prinn: aristocratic woman with square neckline, intricate Elder Sign necklace, long sleeves with embroidered cuffs. In one hand, she holds a "winged eye" symbol; in the other, a human heart,

with her eyes fixed upon it. Vines are coiling around the edges of her illustration as she sits at a writing desk cluttered with miniature cauldrons and apothecary bottles.

    a. Both woodcuts are extraordinary for their level of detail and uniqueness.

        a.i. These woodcuts are contrary to McKerrow's supposition that Early Modern printers preferred woodcuts out of which they could "get their money's worth" from repeated use.

        a.ii. These decorations are too specific to be commonly used in other printmaking projects.

        a.iii. Septimia Prinn's eyes are no longer fixed upon the human heart but are staring straight ahead, engaging with the gaze of the reader.

            — I specifically recorded that her eyes were fixed on the human heart in her hand and I have verified that there are no other reproductions of her portrait in this edition. Despite my headache, I maintain that her eyes have shifted position.

            — Must research Early Modern optical illusion printing techniques.

    b. While there are no records of an Early Modern printer by the name of Elizabeth Breedlove, there are records of Septimia Prinn.

        b.i. Septimia Prinn was the alleged daughter of Ludwig Prinn, a notorious medieval sorcerer and "doctor" of nature, although he did not practice medicine in the traditional sense. He sought to apply his chemical skills to preparing concoctions in "the manner recommended by Paracelsus." Ludwig Prinn is reported to have lived among the wizards and alchemists of England, Germany and Syria, studying everything from divination and rituals of necromancy to blood rites for "the worm that sought to devour the world." He allegedly recorded this forbidden knowledge in a single blasphemous text, establishing his magico-mystical reputation with De Vermis Mysteriis (Mysteries of the Worm).

            — There are rumors that Prinn was a shapeshifter, that Ludwig and Septimia are, in fact, the same person.

It is postulated that, after De Vermis Mysteriis gained popularity, Ludwig's life was endangered by rival cultist factions, so he shifted sexes and identities, and became Septimia, who claimed to be Ludwig's daughter so she could factions, so he shifted sexes and identities, and became continue to draw upon the influence her previous incarnation had acquired.

— I feel like I'm being watched.

b.ii. As Ludwig before her, Septimia Prinn is said to have lived for hundreds of years, moving around Europe, eventually emigrating to the New World, where she is reputed to have given birth to Abigail Prinn, later executed in Salem for witchcraft.

b.iii. Septimia is responsible for hundreds of occult texts found in arcane libraries across the world, although scholars postulate that cultists assumed the name of Septimia Prinn as part of an initiation rite and published under her name; no such postulations are ascribed to Ludwig's writings.

— Someone just whispered in my ear.

— I have been silent for fifteen minutes, my hands off the keyboard, straining my ears to hear anything that could be construed as whispering, but there have been no more whispers.

b.iv. Could E.B. (Elizabeth Breedlove) and Septimia Prinn be the same person?

— Who is H. Vondrak?

b.v. This text was an economic printing; using octavo format, only a few full pages of vellum are needed to produce a single copy. But the woodcuts would've been extravagantly priced for the period. This was printed during the English Civil War, during the trial and execution of Charles I and exile of Charles II. It stands to reason that it would have been sacrilegious to investigate occultism at this time. The small size of this book also indicates a secretive printing. Did Breedlove adopt the pseudonym of Septimia Prinn to absolve herself of responsibility should her press come under

investigation for printing pagan texts?
— Further study into provenance necessary.

Conclusions Regarding *De Deabus Minoribus Exterioris Theomagicae*:
1. I had what I can only call a lucid dream of a tree woman
   caressing my hair with vines, while a quivering octopoid mass
   communicated with me by means I do not understand. We spoke,
   though neither of us used verbal language. I understood that I was being
   asked to give my consent -- for what I do not rightly know. Having
   suffered from sleep paralysis in dreams past, I know I did not feel frozen,
   but rather, felt an active symbiosis of worship and supplication as I
   suckled at the teat of a goat mother and allowed a dream witch to kiss
   the essence of my soul out through my open lips. I understood I was
   being coronated and, in so doing, willfully shed my human skin.
   Underneath, I was a giant worm -- although a worm is much too
   generous a phrase. A maggot is more appropriate, or perhaps a grub,
   although I was so much more majestic. I was craven with a hunger so
   sharp and bright that I knew if I were to devour the universe, not even
   then would I be sated.
   a. When I opened my eyes, my limbs felt foreign to me and
      echoes of chants in unknown languages reverberated in my brain.
   b. Took the bus downtown to campus. I lost a couple of fingers
      along the way. At first, the hum of the bus matched the vibration
      I felt reverberating from inside my body. I felt so centered
      spiritually that, when my pinky finger on my left hand fell off
      and rolled away under a seat, losing it didn't bother me. Even
      the pungent musk of rot that emanated from in its place did not
      bother me, although it was clear that it bothered the other
      passengers as they covered their faces and moved closer to the
      doors.
   c. My ring finger fell off sometime between getting off the bus
      and the library. I only noticed it wasn't there when I lifted my
      hand to buzz the Special Collections room.
      c.i. I had this vague notion that this was troublesome, but
           invocations to the Lesser Outer Goddesses are the only
           things that truly matter to me now.
   d. When Carlo buzzed me into Special Collections, I was suddenly
      overcome with the sharpest, brightest hunger -- so close to the

kind of hunger I knew in my dream. Remembering as much, I asked Carlo if he would be so kind as to give me permission to devour him. He said yes. While he offered up his body in humble obsecration, his voice joined the incantations that churned in my mind.

> d.i.   I said I was hungry, but not hungry enough for khakis, so Carlo undressed, revealing an Elder Sign on his chest. It was the sweetest part of him of all.
>
> d.ii.   I am still so hungry. The deadened husk of my once-arm has fallen off as I type with what remains of my right as a record of my glorious and dreadful evolution.
>
> d.iii.   In between the breaks in my skin, I can see a bulbous, purple luminescence pulsing inside.

2.   I am ready to loose myself from this form, but am I ready to devour the world?

> a. My appetite will serve us well: The suffering for you and yours shall end once and for all, and the festering, protoplasmic ache wracking my grub organs will be satisfied. Conflicts the world over will be quieted as we become one. You will experience the exquisite, sepulchral stillness of oblivion; Humanity united together for the first, and final, time deep within my bowels as the omnipotent waste of the world.
>
> b. And my hunger will be alleviated.
>
> c. I will only proceed with your consent. And know that, as punishment for my appetite, the Lesser Outer Goddesses shall suck the soul marrow from what remains of my diabolical folly— and the world shall be made yet again.
>
> d. If you deny me this indulgence, I will move on to the next world, for there are many. But know that, given a choice, this is the world I would remake; for I am not divorced entirely of my humanity. Although I no longer have need for it in my soon-form, I want to be one with the most fabulous and most profane embodiment of the beautiful chaos of the cosmos.
>
> e. What say you?
>
>> e.i.   May I have your permission to devour the world?

COSMIC ICE EMPRESS

I'm not your fucking star mother.
If you prick me, I bleed black magic.

I am not your fucking goddess of abundance.
I've lived a mortal life of scarcity, the same as you.

I am not your fucking cornucopia of unconditional love.
Nothing about me is endless.

Maybe it was my way with spring that caught your eye.
I have the ability to nurse dead things back to health
because of my preternatural ability for loving things hard enough
they feel it through the decay. My garden was lovely and fecund,
the kind that makes you want to lay between a woman's legs
in the thick, mermaid green grass.

But I have no interest in tending the garden of my mind
in addition to tending the garden of yours.
If I offer you the occasional apple or chrysalis,
it was created from the labor of my own harvest.

If I give, it is because I know what it is to want.

I'm not sure where you learned to take instead of give.
I'm not sure when you learned to feel entitled to open the gate.
I'm not sure when you learned to expect me to say
yes,

of course,
okay,
instead of
no,
not now,
go away.
You cut the flowers and did not plant seeds.
You played at wanting to give, when all you wanted was to receive.

✸

You claimed you had no expectations of me.

✸

Well, let's see how your love of spring handles the winter breeze.

THE GIRL WITH A TASTE
FOR SKELETON KEYS

In an extravagant cage lived a girl with a hole in her heart. The cage was large, much larger than most. The bars of the cage were finely wrought: vaguely Victorian and black iron. Fine enough for a songbird or a phoenix, but a girl with auburn hair, a broken heart, and memories of elsewhere lived there. It was an awful reminder for the ones who walked past her: the passerby avoided catching her gaze for fear that cages were contagious. If the people who did look at her thought about the girl at all, they assumed the girl had been born in the cage. In truth, she had been there so long she had forgotten she had locked herself inside in the first place.

Although the cage scared off most, on occasion, a rare individual would approach the cage and interact with the girl. The bars of the cage were placed just so that the girl could pass pieces of her heart through to the ones who were brave enough to receive a piece. When a passerby accepted a piece of her heart, they mistook the gift for generosity and were touched by what they perceived to be the selflessness of the gesture. But the girl didn't share her heart pieces out of generosity; she did so, rather, out of a selfish desire to forget the pit of loneliness in the middle. With every piece she gave away, the hole in her heart reduced in equal measure.

The girl mistook this progress for healing, presuming that, since the hole in her heart was shrinking, she must be doing something right by giving pieces of it away. Ignoring the fact that her heart as a whole was disappearing along with the crevasse, she continued on in this fashion.

After receiving a shard of her heart, the passerby would try to reciprocate in kind and offer to release her from the cage. Some even had access to diamond-tipped drills and could free her in two shakes of a lamb's tail.

But the girl always declined the offers to leave.

After being rebuffed, the passerby, feeling helpless, would ask whatever happened to the key for the lock? The girl honestly told them that there had been a key years ago, but she swallowed it whole—using her tears to wash it down—and, ever since, the tears and the iron weighed heavily enough in her belly to keep from ever feeling hungry.

Sometimes, if the passerby was particularly clever, they would ask the girl, "Is it better to be hungry or lonely?"

The girl never knew the answer, but she would ponder the question long after it was asked.

One day, a zookeeper came upon the girl in the cage, and seeing an opportunity to add an exquisite exhibit to his zoo, he strolled up to the girl in the cage. He complimented the girl living there, saying the cage was very fine indeed, and the girl, herself, was even finer still. He asked her if she would like him to move the cage to the zoo. There, she would no longer have to live a subsistence lifestyle of relying upon on the scant attention of those not immediately scared off by the wrought iron cage. He promised her that the people who walked by would look at her on purpose, with wonder and fascination, instead of averting their gaze with fear and discomfiture.

The zookeep had heard that the hearts of girls in cages were a delicacy in some parts of the world, and, therefore, he was eager to give hers a taste. If he could also do something good for the zoo as well, so much the better. "I can do all this for the low, low price…of a piece of your heart," he said. "Which you've been passing out willy nilly anyway. So whaddya say? Do we have a deal?"

The zookeep stuck his hand through the bars of the cage offering the girl to shake on it. But the girl hesitated.

After years of breaking off pieces of her heart for others, her heart had grown so small that there wasn't much to break off from anymore. She reckoned she held the last piece right there in her hands. Her fingertips were blackened by years of reaching between the bars—the coal-like dust was thickest there. The girl wanted to allow the zookeeper to relocate her; she wanted to finally be in control of when and where people saw her. She didn't understand how her heart could be so small now, but the pit of loneliness still felt the same.

Something told her that she shouldn't trust this stranger and his offer. And, in addition, she felt as though she couldn't trust herself to not give the last piece of her heart away should the zookeeper be so bold as to ask a second time. She also couldn't trust herself to not blithely offer the last bit of her heart to the next stranger who happened to walk by. So, instead, she curled her inky fingertips around her heart's last piece, politely declined the zookeeper's offer, and swallowed up the last of her heart herself.

"Your loss," the zookeep shrugged and went along his merry way.

The girl wept about giving up such a fine offer; she wept so much that she eventually cried out a skeleton key through her tears.

The girl could feel the rumble in her belly, and, having no use for keys, she almost swallowed the key again to keep the old hunger at bay.

But, instead, she allowed her belly to grumble for the first time in years, and her gut told her to unlock the cage and run as far away from it as she could.

Dearest, do you know what that girl did?

She listened to her gut. She unlocked that cage.

As soon as she was about to step one foot outside the cage, though, the girl froze. The abject fear of not knowing what life could look like beyond the cage paralyzed her. So, she snapped the cage door shut once more and locked herself inside with the key she had made in her own belly.

And she swallowed the key.

Of course, now the girl has forgotten that a key ever existed, or that a key can possibly exist; she has also forgotten that she has the power to make the key herself. Instead, she loves to hate that beautiful, wretched cage. It's not wrong that the girl missed the confines of the cage before she could step even one foot outside it. It's to be expected, really.

My hope is that, one day, she will give herself permission to have an insatiable appetite that can't be satisfied by keys she forgot she swallowed. My hope is that, one day, she feasts for a thousand years on vinyl records, tintype photographs, Egyptian tombs, and the mouths of filmmakers and poets.

But my secret hope is that, one day, when I am old and gray and dying on a bed, she will take a spoon and sample the sky and tell me how it tastes, calling upon the palate she's developed from that insatiable appetite of hers. And there she will brush my hair aside and kiss my forehead and let me die happy knowing she finally found a way to live without needing a cage at all.

VOID SETUP (SACKVILLEWEST) LOOP

~~I am a thing.~~
I am reduced to a thing that wants Virginia.
—Vita Sackville-West

January 21
Harmony Mills, NY
I imagine her mouth to be like ink and her lips would tattoo kisses upon my skin. Ink is a precious commodity at Harmony Mills, and I feel as though I would know what it must be to be a real writer, and not just a skinbag of gears and ligaments with a ghost attached; if only Virginia were to write her story across my body with her lips.

On second thought … I would be her text.

A limited edition volume.

January 22
We are not supposed to know each other's names in here. In fact, it is verboten.

Virginia taught me that word.

And when Virginia taught me that word, and confessed her name, 'V' became my favorite letter.

January 23
Harmony Mills
Her loom was next to mine. I would watch as she wove her narrative fabric

with fingers too nimble. Her grace a constant reminder of how clumsy my own narrative handiwork is—imperfections in the strands.

I am merely a grub next to her delicate spidery.

It was her hands I fell in love with first. With those hands, she wove together a galaxy that only the two of us could navigate.

And for a time, I forgot the other girls, all hunched over and plugged into their machines. For a time, the sound of looms and keys was like dandelion tufts on the air.

I had a dream that my name was Alice
And your name was Charles.
I asked you to tell me a story.
You wrote one,
Starring me in the Under Ground.
You pat my head,
Gave me a kerchief.
I let you snip a lock of my hair.

You said:
> *Victorians made*
> *Memento mori*
> *Out of the hair of loved ones.*

Dead loved ones, I said.

You told me to nevermind that,
Hair does not spoil and
Thus is immortal.
Unlike our bodies.
> *But I want to be mortal*
> *With your body.*

I want to know what it is to hold you
Through gaslamp and fog.
> *-- V*

How did you find this notebook?

You keep it under your pillow – as
though you wish to fill it by osmosis.
If anyone could will such a thing,
it would be you.

Considering this place is a necarium of ghosts attached to a combination of
biomatter and cybernetic components, I am not sure if undead things can have a
will.

You give life to this necrotized place. And for this reason, I shall call you Vita.

I wish I could remember my life from before.

Why? That life is over. We are together now.

February 13
I dreamt that I liked her better in knickers. She had more movement that
way. We were human and she could do cartwheels and her hair glowed in the
sunlight. She laughed when she was in knickers. And sometimes you would start
to float away, but there was a ribbon tied around your waist for just such an
occasion.

You were my Alice Kite.

Your laugh was a full, round sound, like a cannon that fired cloud aether, and,
losing yourself in the moment, would begin to levitate.

But I was always there. The height of me would attach to the slim breadth of
you. You were all angles in the sunlight, something that I needed to steer.

Once, in the red rose garden, I pulled you down out of the sky, after you had
laughed at my inability to cartwheel—I hadn't taken off my overcoat or even
emptied my pockets, so the cartwheel was doomed from the start—you began to
float skyward.

As I caught hold of that ribbon tethered round your waist, I saw you see the blueness of my eyes. I saw you wonder if I would kiss you. You wondered what it might be like. The question, "What do lips upon lips feel like?" was resonant across your face.

Curioser and curioser, your wonder began to bend around the idea of my mouth, if I'd wait until both of your feet were firmly planted on solid ground.

You hoped I wouldn't wait.

How did your dream end?

It is a known fact that when two people both want something at the same exact moment, it is inevitable that decorum will overcome desire.

So I kissed you instead.

You did.

You did. How many ways are there to cage a butterfly?

Why would you want to cage one at all?

She loved him with what he thought was a child's affection, when in truth, she loved him with a child's fierceness. She loved with a certain kind of immortality only achievable before one's first heartbreak.

It was his hands, at first, in which she fell in love.

They were ink-stained. Even though she had never seen a sailor covered in tattoos, she imagined him as such. Should she be brave enough to raise his cuff, she wanted to find the ink wrapping up around his arms, and since she was being brave, she would find the ink extended to his chest and shoulders, binding his skin in the shape of an octopus that covered his body in a secret only she would know.

She imagined him a pirate, save for his sea was made of inkwells, and the jars and bottles would clatter on the tide.

She imagined his ship made of paper, and his pirate flag wouldn't be a skull and crossbones, but typography which read: "Dirty, wild things." He'd raise that flag on his way to her, and navigate by a compass that always pointed to her as true north.

She wanted to know what it was to be pillaged, should he be the one doing the pillaging.

--V

Why am I a man in our dreams?

Remnants of a previous life.

Charles.
Orlando.
Vita.

Variations on a theme.

He loved her with what she thought was a frustrating politeness, which she took to mean that he was capable of only loving her in pieces, when in truth, he loved her to the height and width and breadth of his soul.

He loved with a certain kind of trepidation only achievable after one's heart has been broken. The broken prism of his previous experience refracted, magnified and threw into sharp relief a spectrum of love that he didn't know existed before her.

It was her eyes, at first, maybe second, which he fell in love with. They were lit with green fire. Whenever he lost sight of her, all he had to do was close his eyes and follow the green embers that she left in her wake. He imagined there was a dragon living inside her chest, breathing fire and light when she was running and laughing, the kind of light that filled her up and made her start to levitate and float away.

When he told her that he loved her, but that he was too old for her, and that when she grew up and married a nice young man her own age, she would forget about him, and that's the way it should be, he knew there was a dragon in her breast, breathing brimstone and ash.

He didn't want to tame the dragon that nestled there, he wanted to free it.

I love you in spite of being turned into a haunted phonograph.

Days after we pass this notebook contraband, the echoes of your writing remain and hang in my brain.

I wish I could simply turn the needle and change the tune, for the way you haunt my thoughts clouds my craftsmanship. And it's bad enough that we are in possession of a connection that is more powerful than either of us could anticipate—but that we are creating a story together.

If this gets in the way of the commissions, we'll be rebooted. But I love you with an all-consuming selfishness that precludes even your safety. So my love is colored by a certain kind of guilt—that shouldn't your safety be my first priority if I love you in the way that I claim?

I fear that I am simply addicted to our brand of theater.

We have created a play where we each get to truly be ourselves in our current incarnation.

Dearest Creature,

Make
an
outlaw
of
me.
—Vita

You silly, wondrous spirit. They will come looking for your key.

If you are a haunted phonograph, I am now turned into a deep-sea diver for sunken treasure.

My evidence is three-fold, as good evidence always is.

Item the first:
I am the perfect territory for sharks and mermaids.

Mermaids are often in disguise.

But so are sharks.

Being open in the face of being bitten is the scariest place to be.

Item the second:

Looking for sunken treasure helps me put my cartography skills to good use. You, Virginia, are an explorer. I'm just the cartographer trying to keep pace.

You have faith that there's not an edge to the world: that the world is full and round and we won't fall off of it.

At least, that was how you used to believe. Somehow, along the way, I absorbed your faith—most likely, through some form of vampirism, and it has become a part of me. Lines and maps are everywhere and nowhere all at once and I see the world as a web of interconnectedness—that surely if a predator were to strike upon the web we have become entangled upon, your spider hands would feel the sensations on the strands.

Item the third:
If you're a haunted phonograph, then that qualified as sunken treasure and I found you.

I wanted to be plugged into you. Download your storyline. Cut it up. And paste the shapes of dolls and girls and flying objects into this notebook.

They are
looking for
your key.

卌 卌 卌 卌 卌 卌 卌 卌 卌 卌 卌 卌 卌 卌 卌 卌 卌 卌 卌
卌 卌 卌 卌 卌 卌 卌 卌 卌 卌 卌 卌 卌 卌 卌 卌 卌 卌 卌
卌 卌 卌 卌 卌 卌 卌 卌 卌 卌 卌 卌 卌 卌 卌 卌 卌 卌 卌
卌 卌 卌 卌 卌 卌 卌 卌 卌 卌 卌 卌 卌 卌 卌 卌 卌 卌 卌
卌 卌 卌 卌 卌 卌 卌 卌 卌 卌 卌 卌 卌 卌 卌 卌 卌 卌 卌
卌 卌 卌 卌 卌 卌 卌 卌 卌 卌 卌 卌 卌 卌 卌 卌 卌 卌 卌
卌 卌 卌 卌 卌 卌 卌 卌 卌 卌 卌 卌 卌 卌 卌 卌 卌 卌 卌
卌 卌 卌 卌 卌 卌 卌 卌 卌 卌 卌 卌 卌 卌 卌 卌 卌 卌 卌
卌 卌 卌 卌 卌 卌 卌 卌 卌 卌 卌 卌 卌 卌 卌 卌 卌 卌 卌
卌 卌 卌 卌 卌 卌 卌 卌 卌 卌 卌 卌 卌 卌 卌 卌 卌 卌 卌
卌 卌 卌 卌 卌 卌 卌 卌 卌 卌 卌 卌 卌 卌 卌 卌 卌 卌 卌
卌 卌 卌 卌 卌 卌 卌 卌 卌 卌 卌 卌 卌 卌 卌 卌 卌 卌 卌
卌 卌 卌 卌 卌 卌 卌 卌 卌 卌 卌 卌 卌 卌 卌 卌 卌 卌 卌
卌 卌 卌 卌 卌 卌 卌 卌 卌 卌 卌 卌 卌 卌 卌 卌 卌 卌 卌
卌 卌 卌 卌 卌 卌 卌 卌 卌 卌 卌 卌 卌 卌 卌 卌 卌 卌 卌
卌 卌 卌 卌 卌 卌 卌 卌 卌 卌 卌 卌 卌 卌 卌 卌 卌 卌 卌
卌 卌 卌 卌 卌 卌 卌 卌 卌 卌 卌 卌 卌 卌 卌 卌 卌 卌 卌
卌 卌 卌 卌 卌 卌 卌 卌 卌 卌 卌 卌 卌 卌 卌 卌 卌 卌 卌
卌 卌 卌 卌 卌 卌 卌 卌 卌 卌 卌 卌 卌 卌 卌 卌 卌 卌 卌
卌 卌 卌 卌 卌 卌 卌 卌 卌 卌 卌 卌 卌 卌 卌 卌 卌 卌 卌
卌 卌 卌 卌 卌 卌 卌 卌 卌 卌 卌 卌 卌 卌 卌 卌 卌 卌 卌
卌 卌 卌 卌 卌 卌 卌 卌 卌 卌 卌 卌 卌 卌 卌 卌 卌 卌 卌
卌 卌 卌 卌 卌 卌 卌 卌 卌 卌 卌 卌 卌 卌 卌 卌 卌 卌 卌
卌 卌 卌 卌 卌 卌 卌 卌 卌 卌 卌 卌 卌 卌 卌 卌 卌 卌 卌
卌 卌 卌 卌 卌 卌 卌 卌 卌 卌 卌 卌 卌 卌 卌 卌 卌 卌 卌
卌 卌 卌 卌 卌 卌 卌 卌 卌 卌 卌 卌 卌 卌 卌 卌 卌 卌 卌
卌 卌 卌 卌 卌 卌 卌 卌 卌 卌 卌 卌 卌 卌 卌 卌 卌 卌 卌
卌 卌 卌 卌 卌 卌 卌 卌 卌 卌 卌 卌 卌 卌 卌 卌 卌 卌 卌
卌 卌 卌 卌 卌 卌 卌 卌 卌 卌 卌 卌 卌 卌 卌 卌 卌 卌 卌
卌 卌 卌 卌 卌 卌 卌 卌 卌 卌 卌 卌 卌 卌 卌 卌 卌 卌 卌
卌 卌 卌 卌 卌 卌 卌 卌 卌 卌 卌 卌 卌 卌 卌 卌 卌 卌 卌
卌 卌 卌 卌 卌 卌 卌 卌 卌 卌 卌 卌 卌 卌 卌 卌 卌 卌 卌
卌 卌 卌 卌 卌 卌 卌 卌 卌 卌 卌 卌 卌 卌 卌 卌 卌 卌 卌
卌 卌 卌 卌 卌 卌 卌 卌 卌 卌 卌 卌 卌 卌 卌 卌 卌 卌 卌
卌 卌 卌 卌 卌 卌 卌 卌 卌 卌 卌 卌 卌 卌 卌 卌 卌 卌 卌
卌 卌 卌 卌 卌 卌 卌 卌 卌 卌 卌 卌 卌 卌 卌 卌 卌 卌 卌

Harmony Mills
They have taken Virginia, but left the notebook.

At one point, I had gotten hold of the pattern of days and figured out what day it was in this factory. But I lost track of the days daydreaming and storytelling and kissing with Virginia.

I must find her.

I feel compelled to continue to record the operation of things should this notebook survive my quest instead of me.

Here, inside the factory, there are hundreds of us. But what are we? We are ghosts of our former selves. It is impossible to tell if I am who I used to be, or if I am simply programmed this way: electrified synapses and cogs in a machine.

Virginia remembered who she was, who she is. And when we were plugged into our storyboards, she would conjure the vestiges of her former life.

Our former life.

She said we each other there.

Downloading a story made us feel closer to each other—in these moments where I write for myself and for Virginia, or even when I am commissioned to produce a story—I feel connected to my previous incarnation, even while I cannot quite remember her. Me? The sensation of writing feels like time travel. As long as I am writing I feel Virginia.

This means she hasn't been rebooted yet.

Harmony Mills
All of us girls have keyholes on our backs. This is where the factory plugs us in to the storyboards, "the looms" we call them; this is where they insert the keys to keep us activated.

This is where they insert the key to deactivate us.

Our original design featured the keyhole on our chests, the second design on our craniums. But some of the girls always managed to make a makeshift key and deactivate themselves.

Powering themselves down was better than being forced to download stories they didn't want to be telling.

When the machine part of us powers down, there's no energy to sustain the soul tethered there.

Virginia told me she had deactivated herself twice before.

Technically, three times, she'd correct herself.

I stole my key because, even though I cannot reach my keyhole without Virginia's help, I want to be in charge of my fate. I gave it to Virginia because I wanted her to know that there is no me without her.

I am running out of pages and ink.

Writing, pen on paper, is the only way I feel connected to Virginia.

It ultimately didn't matter that I stole my key. The factory has replacements. I should've anticipated such a thing. But I still wish I hadn't stolen it some days— the days I don't write, save for the lone scrawl mark that enumerates the day I spent without Virginia and without knowing about Virginia.

My heart is a black hole.

She was a barred and spiral galaxy.

The
    Thread
        Has
            Been
                Cut.

Harmony Mills

When Virginia returned, she returned a blank slate.

I felt the connection between us severed and the next day, she appeared.
Plugged into her storyboard, conjuring and downloading a story for Licensee No.
0714.

Her hands still weave her stories with an unearthly grace.

But the dragon I was sure that lived inside her chest has been released.

Perhaps we just have to keep her hands filled with ink and paper, and, just
the way I used writing—and as the days wore on—spiraling—maybe she'll able to
plot her way back to me.

I am an excellent cartographer, after all.

// end experimental consciousness
// setup initializes subject sackvillewest
// loop checks narrative each time,
// and will send after license activated
// delay reboot for 1825 days

THE PALEOLITHIC VENUSIAN BORN OF JADE TIGER FIRE

The Venusian learned early on that if she allowed her fire to plume and grow, mortals were drawn to her smoke signals. She didn't mind sharing her particular shade of jade green flames with them at first, for she understood the magic exclusive to fire: that it is not diminished when halved and shared, but, instead, is increased. The more she split her fire in two, the more fire there was for the having.

But, then, one day, a rogue appeared on the horizon; he had been drawn to the shapes in the smoke her fire made. Taking pity on his bedraggled heart, she shared her fire with him so it might keep and nourish him as it had so many others who had come to her from the horizon.

When the rogue had first encountered her, he had been attracted to the Venusian's volcanic heat and how she wielded it. But, soon, he discovered a valuable side effect of her jade flames. Over the years of sharing and increasing her soulfire, the coals in her heart had turned into diamonds. Being made of fire, the Venusian had no use for diamonds; she did have use of the coals the green fire in her soul survived on—these were the embers she passed on to others so that they might start jade fires of their own. Eventually, though, the rogue grew jealous of the diamonds she managed to forge herself without even trying—he had been starved for so long that he didn't understand that she would've given him the diamonds freely had he but asked.

The rogue couldn't risk the Venusian giving away her riches to those in need, so he made a plan to isolate her from the desert where she conducted her work. He told her that he wanted to breathe her smoke deep down into his lungs, so that she would be a part of his body for always. He told her that he wanted to bathe himself in her flames. He said he wanted the Venusian to forge him with the heat of her body. She was seduced by the beauty and finesse of the rogue's tongue, and she licked his lips with her fire. The Venusian was not married to the desert. She had worked so long and had shared so much of her soulfire that, for once, she could take some time for herself. She willingly invited the rogue to live with her in her home, where they could indulge in the decadence of sharing the kind of naked heat that melts iron into liquid.

Growing impatient for the Venusian to either share the diamonds on her own, or to discard them because she had far too many, the rogue decided to steal some ember diamonds from her cauldron. He placed them in warming pans under his mattress and secretly sold them. With the money, he bought a cottage for them to share—the Venusian's home had been a reminder of her looming responsibilities. He said he wanted to take care of her the way she had taken care of him. But, as she slept on the bed in the house bought with money the rogue stole by stealing the diamonds of her soul, the Venusian began to grow weak. The rogue was willfully ignorant as to why, and took the opportunity to nurse her during her illness. He provided the funds they would need for mystics and medusas to assess her health and prescribe a course of action.

For the final time, the rogue opened the cauldron. He sifted through variegated tendrils of the Venusian's green flames looking for a gem, but the rogue grew panicked to find the coals of her heart dying out as he searched.

Maybe the rogue didn't realize that by stealing the tinder for the bonfire of her soul meant her heart grew colder with every theft of coal. Maybe he didn't realize the extent of his theft because, at one time, she freely gave away her flames. And she never regretted giving them away so freely because she understood the rules of her innate fire magic: that by sharing the flames, they only grew stronger and doubled in size.

But sharing fire is not the same as it being stolen. Sharing fire, the Venusian was careful to keep the embers in her heart burning brightly. She nurtured and fed those flames with the gristle of grimoires and the meat of poets. She coaxed her green fire until it was luminous as sunlight and sharp as lightning. But when the rogue stole her fire and flames, he had not been careful to leave enough fire to both power herself as well as to share.

Even though the Venusian is ancient amongst mortals, she's was just a maiden amongst her own ancient kind. She did not understand how there was no longer enough fire in her heart to go around.

The fire in her heart was hungry, but the rogue left her nothing with which to feed it.

The rogue was restless—constantly checking the cauldron for diamonds made as a side effect of the Venusian's work. It wasn't long before she was down to the last soulfire spark, and as the fire burnt out, a tiny diamond formed, white-hot with the possibility of starting another forge for the Venusian's soul. It was then that the rogue asked for her final ember. Even though she knew better than to do it, she gave him the last glowing ember of her djinniyeh fire in the hopes that he might choose to share the fire back with her, as she had shared with him when he came to her from the desert horizon.

Warmth in the body is life itself; it's our own form of biological fire, and when that fire dies, our bodies go cold. And even though mortals and the Venusian are made of entirely different stuff, we all are powered by sources of heat. As the warmth left her body, the rogue left her without so much as a spark to rekindle the flames of her heart.

And so, her heart and body entombed themselves in ice, until there was a glacier between her and the world.

And there she dreamed of candles and incense and bundles of sage. She dreamed of ofrendas and pan de muertos. She dreamed of matches and match-books and constellations, of wishes written on paper and burned in flames, of the firebird, of ashes, of sparks plugs and pistons. She dreamed until she ignited her own heart once again. She dreamed until the fire that burns brightest in both her heart and her belly cracked the glacier straight down the center, and she was born again in smokeless fire.

She emerged a tigress made of green flame and striped with shadows. She was reborn starving for all forms of ignition.

She embraced her appetite. She allowed ritualists to dance before her exquisite flames, and then devoured their tattooed skin and invocations to higher powers. Soldiers with cowboy accents and blue eyes defended her lustful honor. She sampled every form of light and power, shadow and spark, the universe has to offer.

And when she was full, she took one spoonful more.

The Venusian filled her djinniyeh heart with so much love and lust, with so much devotion and desire, that her light and her appetite consumed the horizon.

She had been starved for far too long.

STAR WOLF

I am a wolf made of swirling galaxies and I am in search of a pack. The constant search for wolves made of similar stuff has been wearisome on my wolf bones. The pads of my wolf feet are dry and cracked from miles of searching in the snow—snow that goes on for infinity in all three dimensions of cubic volume. So it comes as no surprise that the trails I once found have long since grown cold. It comes as no surprise that I have lost the scent of creatures made of the same star stuff as me.

But then there is a crow. He is white as the snow I trudge through, and I can tell he relishes the surprise he causes me by undermining my expectations of what a crow should look like. I don't think it's unreasonable to expect a crow to be made of the same density of blackness as myself. The crow enjoys the way he stands out in the murder of other crows—at once, accepted as part of the collective, but also singular in his peculiar color.

My heart is made of dark matter, and its comes with its own gravitational pull, and although the crow is curious about my orbit, he is wary as well. And he should be. I am made of the crushing force of a thousand collapsed suns. What creature could possibly withstand the catastrophic force of a star running out of fuel and condensing into a black hole shaped like a wolf?

It is better to not be curious about such creatures. It is best to make my bed in the snow and sleep and sink into an event horizon of my own making.

But the crow's curiosity follows me, outweighing his natural impulse of wariness. He makes wide circles at first, creating his own apogean path, giving me time to decide whether I trust the crow to come any closer, giving him time to decide whether he trusts my jaws to be still.

I stay still. I don't snap my teeth. I don't even howl, even though the moon is bright and full, and I can feel her yanking on the tides of the planets that swirl inside me. The moon makes me want to run; not in fear, but to run for the joyful crunch of paws on snow—and my particular ability to melt into the night.

When the crow swoops toward me, he is conjunction with my heart and flies right through. He isn't bound by my gravity. He isn't bound by the orbital path I would've expected my dark-matter-heart to force upon other creatures who dared to venture too close. The diving conjunction gives the crow his own momentum, and he flies the highest I have ever seen a crow fly. So high that the moon is able to lean down and give the crow a kiss, and moonbeams bounce off of his back.

Seeing him fly in such a way gives me hope that I, too, can survive as a star wolf, with swirling galaxies—even without a pack to call my own.

THE HURRICANE BOTTLE

Various methods of water witching have been employed to find The Woman Made of Water over the years. Dowsing rods, pendulums, and even the occasional tarot card have been used to scry for her exact location. When found, most are only interested in replicating her peculiar chemistry, such as her unique covalence of hydrogen and carbon representing the building blocks of life, the universe, and everything. Since her pure nature has been taken advantage of so often during the course of her existence, she tries very hard not to be found, and, instead, works to do the finding.

Once, hundreds of years ago, philosophers and doctors of the four humors recognized that people who had an overabundance of water in their bodies tended to be quiet and reserved, with large doses of apathy. These people were categorized as *phlegmatic*. But they had to invent an entirely new word for The Woman Made of Water, seeing as how she was made entirely of the stuff that unbalanced humans into a variety of lethargies. She thought of herself as *fluidus*, and argued as such, but they offered to label her as *indecisus*, so she ran away from the philosophers of nature.

As time moved forward, The Woman Made of Water was sought out as a source of creativity. Particularly during the Romantic period, artists, poets, and spiritual leaders alike saw her potential for being bottled and sold as indulgences across the continent. Drops of her could be commercialized as wards against droughts of inspiration, divine or otherwise. The Woman Made of Water was willing to appease these demands upon her time and attention because she loved humans so. Her love was so strong that she struck a deal with Biology, offering to compose a majority of our bodies' elements. In exchange, she would nurture humans as her creation and would provide for us as such. But, over time, humans grew to favor a Divine Watchmaker over The Woman Made of Water, as self-made mechanisms were very "in" during those years after the Romantic era.

Once, not even that long ago, the Navy figured out that they could use The Woman Made of Water to power jet engines—her potential as an endless source of energy, they were convinced, should be used for industry, and The Woman Made of Water knew that industry would be warring. The Navy tried to convince her that there were other applicable uses for jet fuel aside from powering drones or fighter jets, but The Woman Made of Water refused. What the Navy did not understand was that all of the universe, each individual particle, is cherished by her, so The Woman Made of Water could not abide the Navy using electricity to separate her into her most basic elements in a form of proprietary fusion. And so, she again ran.

The Woman Made of Water overflows with the potential energy of the universe. She is the cauldron of life and the soul-shrine that holds the spirit in place to prevent it from dissipating into ether. Within her, dreams manifest into reality. But, the kind of endless external searching for her by philosophers, artists, and the Navy are not necessary—one only has to remember that our bodies are mostly composed of water.

She encourages the ones who manage to remember to practice the fine art of surrender, not as in a laying down of arms, but as a way of allowing water to carve out the paths of riverbeds in the mountains of our souls.

The Woman Made of Water reminds us about the need for unconditional receiving, as she, herself, has been a vessel that overflows with both passion and compassion. She says these overflow like the Nile during Ahket, the Season of Inundation. She says where water flows, fertile ground is left behind for us to till as we see fit; however, she says, a note of gentle warning in her voice, it's important to remember that we are ultimately responsible for the tending of our own growing grounds.

One day, she came upon The Rider trying to fly. He was nowhere near an ocean, and, so, was practicing sailing on the wind with a bicycle he had fitted with wings made out of wax and goddess feathers. But his bicycle wasn't flying so much as it was flailing, and since The Woman Made of Water is an expert at fluidity, she offered to help.

"I don't think I'm good enough to fly," The Rider said.

"Who tells you you're unworthy of flight?" The Woman Made of Water asked.

The Rider was quiet a moment as he considered her question. To be true, it was the echo of the things his heart had said in the past that rang through him now, clear through down to the toes of his soul. "My heart," he said, looking away from her, ashamed.

"Your heart sounds like a silly creature. I wouldn't listen to its nonsense," she replied, in what was probably an annoying, wise tone of voice. Being ancient the way she was, The Woman Made of Water did not always understand how some advice is sometimes too obvious, or too useless, to say out loud.

The Rider replied, "My heart says I'm going to be a terrible flyer. And why should I try if I'm going to terrible?"

The Woman Made of Water touched her hand under The Rider's chin and lifted his face so his eyes would meet hers, which were made of night water and swirling nebulas. "Who said you had to be good on the first try?"

The Rider rubbed his chin, wiping the dripping water from his face where she had touched him. The nearness of The Woman Made of Water was at once alternating current and the coolness of the wind off the surface of a soda lake. It can be difficult for an earthling creature to understand anything based in water the way she is—unless the earthling learns the value of surrender.

He couldn't bear to look her in the eye, so he looked down at his shoes as he asked, "Would you help me?"

The Rider's wave of vulnerability crashed over her, and compassion welled inside her molecules and bade her to take him to The Workshop.

The Workshop was arranged with the utmost care and attention to the kind of logic only found in dreams. There were piles of objects preternaturally arranged and stacked in such intricate, interlocking ways, that to remove a small object seemingly unconnected to the integrity of the structure would surely send the objects spilling to the floor and crashing into other piles.

The Rider was drawn to one precarious stack that contained dozens of white baby teeth, skeleton keys, a Commodore 64 with a VGA monitor, 8" floppy disks, a dot matrix printer, a left sneaker, a right sneaker with the bones of a foot still in it, two rotary phones, a telegraph, a typewriter, a specimen jar that contained four wisdom teeth, an articulated cat skeleton, a Walkman, copper pennies, a pair of finely embroidered golden lotus slippers, square nails, incandescent light bulbs, a wicker basket, alkaline batteries, roller skates, a small plastic case containing twenty-four cake decorating tips, a Japanese phrasebook, bricks of postmarked envelopes bound together with rubber bands, and a hardback copy of *Watership Down*.

"When a recipe calls for something abandoned, I pull ingredients from this pile," The Woman Made of Water said. There was a cobalt blue bottle smack dab in the middle of the stack of objects, and, as she reached up for it, her watery limbs extended to reach the height.

"Oh no!" The Rider yelped.

"It's an exercise in centeredness," she said as she managed to lift the bottle right out of the middle of the pile without so much as clinking it against the side of the metal eggbeater that rested above it. Inside, a miniature hurricane roared with thunder and lightning and tiny raindrops scattered the inside of the glass.

"What are you going to do with it?" The Rider asked.

"I'm going to transfer your heart to this jar, and move this hurricane from here," she pointed to the bottle, "to there." She pointed to his chest.

Heart transplants are usually a bloody process for earthlings, unless they're lucky enough for their surgeons to be ancient mythological creatures. The Woman Made of Water took a pen and drew a square on The Rider's chest, where his heart should be. She then drew a little doorknob and turned the handle she had just drawn on his chest, and the square of flesh opened freely. With silver scissors, she cut the threads connecting The Rider's heart to his insides. He could feel the tension of the thread against the blades of the scissors, the distinctive, muted pops of threads snapping reverberated in his body. As The Woman Made of Water removed The Rider's heart with one hand, she replaced the space in his chest with the hurricane from the bottle with her other. Once it was secure, she softly closed the door, the seams in The Rider's skin healing into clean flesh. He could feel a not unpleasant hum from the hurricane throughout his whole body.

"Now your heart can no longer whisper vicious nothings in your mind," she said.

And this is how The Rider learned the art of surrender.

The Woman Made of Water took The Rider to a cliff, and he explored the edges with his toes. Even though the believable fictions his heart had whispered to him remained in his brain like echoes in a hospital hallway, the storm brewing in his chest encouraged him to take his contraption and jump.

There really was nothing left to do but to do the thing he had set out to do. So The Rider did.

And he fell.

He and his hybrid bicycle aviation machine fell for a very long time. He thought about apples and rabbit holes. He thought about falling in love and falling into truth. He thought about his heart and wondered if it could feel the force of gravity carrying him down with increasing velocity. He thought of the waxed and feathered wings almost too late to experience their great gift of flight.

He rode the air bike back up to the plateau where The Woman Made of Water watched him soar.

When he saw her, The Rider remembered that, for a moment, he had been brave enough to admit being scared, and The Woman Made of Water had treated that vulnerability with compassion. As he rode in the air above her, he came to realize that when he had jumped his wax-winged bicycle off the cliff, he had fallen in love with her.

He landed his bike next to her on the edge of the cliff. "I want to give you something as lovely as what you've given me."

The Woman Made of Water was astounded. She had learned long ago that generosity had never been the strong suit of earthling creatures, and, through the years, she had come to forgive them for using her for inspiration; for power struggles; for never replenishing the supply from which they had taken. She forgave their greed because she understood dehydration and thirst make people desperate. So The Rider's desire for reciprocity was unknown to her, and she didn't quite know what to make of it.

"With the hurricane now inside my chest, there is a kiss of wind and water inside me that make me understand what it is like to churn with a power strong enough to flood whole cities in a single wave. I recognize now that you have the ability to submerge a township under water by calling upon your power—and yet you do not. You could rip a two-thousand-year-old sequoia up by the roots should it be your will—but you would never wield your power in such a way."

The Woman Made of Water was the forgiving and patient sort; she had to be. As much as she could forgive humans for being greedy creatures, over time, she managed to convince herself that she didn't need to be acknowledged as a force in peoples' lives—that she gave her energy away freely and that the bodies she nourished did not have an obligation to repay her for her attention. Once or twice, she had wished she could have been a minor god, demanding tithes in gratitude for the bounties she provided. But, for the power of surrender to truly work and enrich the lives of those she touched, she had to balance a specific combination of erosion and waiting.

"You understand me in a way that no one else had been able to fathom before," she said, and her eyes became watery with tears. She handed him the pen she had used for his open-heart surgery, and The Rider jumped his bike into the sky and began drawing jellyfish floating through the air as he rode past. He illustrated all the different kinds of jellyfish he had read about in books, making clouds of moon jellies, medusas, and man o' wars.

The Woman Made of Water had never seen such imaginative play between air and water.

As she watched The Rider turn the sky into his own personal canvas for her amusement, The Woman Made of Water thought about how she had made a happy enough existence for herself, nurturing a natural fluidity in others through the centuries. She was never lonely because she felt connected to all of human-kind through the water in our bodies and souls. Even though she had existed for thousands of years, even though she knew all the different ways to wear down a mountain—including scrubbing with steel wool, as well as singing a mournful tune that lasted at least seven-hundred-sixty-thousand years—she never had the desire to mix water with air. That was the business of other water gods and creatures, but not for her. She had never wanted anything to do with air. She knew she couldn't exactly exist without it on some molecular level, but that was as far as her fascination with air went.

But then, a moon jelly drifted down toward her on the breeze, and The Woman Made of Water cupped it into her hands, and the moon jelly slipped into the water of her palms and floated up her wrists and arms and settled into her chest, where it glowed with its own soft fuchsia bioluminescence. And she knew then that she loved The Rider the way you know when you read a poem, and it becomes written on your soul, and you fall in love with Emily Dickinson a little more every time you read her work, and, regardless of how many years it's been since she took her last breath, her work lingers and haunts the corridors of your mind, and you keep her as a welcome ghost there.

The Woman Made of Water never rightly understood surrender until she came to know The Rider. She thought she had known, but, really, she came to understand that the surrendering had all been on behalf of the mountain she was conquering, or the glacier she was melting, or the bodies that were being formed by seventy percent of her. One must surrender enough to receive, as well as to give.

As much as she would have preferred The Rider grow gills and make a home inside of her so she could carry him with her wherever she went, she could never take The Rider's wax-winged bicycle away from him. She knew he would always be partially married to the air. At first, she cursed her watery heart for loving such an air-based animal; but there finally came a day when she stopped cursing her heart and basked in the beauty of his flight. And that was the day she finally came to understand the value of surrender.

It is said that The Woman Made of Water thought The Rider most beautiful when he was bicycling the sky.

INHERITED FORMS OF PYROMANCY

Years later, when the mother had a son born with a moon on his leg, she took him into the rainforests of California where the redwoods that dwelled there swelled with rainclouds they made themselves. The magic of the redwoods reminded her of the best kind of magic, and she realized that it was high time to teach her son about the self-made kind.

Beneath a waxing crescent moon, the mother took The Boy With A Moon On His Leg to sit beneath the trees and the stars. She brought a leather and canvas pack with sundries of items for the occasion. She took out the rocks her son had collected from his adventures on top of mountains, and along creeks, and inside parking lots, and with these she created a circle.

Next, she took out books—both hardcover and paperback—along with cassette tapes. Inside the rock circle, Charles Dickens, J. D. Salinger, and Jack Kerouac were placed with care next to The Beatles, U2, and Eric Clapton. The plastic cases were removed, but the paper inserts where chucked together with the books in a campfire lay of cultural kindling. Just as The Boy With A Moon On His Leg was wondering what sort of altar his mother was making in the middle of the woods, she pulled at the spools of the cassettes.

When the magnetic tape was properly splayed in curly spools around the pyramids of books, the mother struck the match she had brought exactly for this occasion and held the hissing thing out to her son.

"This is the flame of discontent," the mother said to her son as she leaned forward, offering him the match.

"You want me to set these on fire?" her son asked, his green eyes flashed in the firelight. He leaned his body away from his mother. He was trying to remember this was the same woman who had built him a temple of books, and after he was nestled inside, had given him a flashlight with which to read Paulo Freire's *Pedagogy of the Oppressed*. This was the same woman who had conjured digital memories of Hendrix and Queen and reminded him that he didn't have to die young in order to be legendary.

"Don't be afraid of the spark of discontent," his mother said. "Nourish the spark until it becomes a roaring flame, until the engine of your soul is powered by an everlasting discontent."

"Most parents are way more subtle about wanting their children to be unhappy," her son said, folding his arms the way he had seen precocious teenagers do in movies.

"What I want for you, my love, is to be discontent with everything. I want you to be discontent with cultural canons. I want you to question who you read and why, and look for the stories no one is telling and listen for the music no one is singing. I want you to be discontent with a culture that colonizes the voices of dissent and then repackages those messages to be less threatening to the status quo. I want you to be discontent with a job that will keep you too busy to notice the injustices that plague your fellow humans. I want you to be bored by prestige, and I want you see through the structures of power. I want you to see. I want you to think. I want you to create. And that can only happen by cultivating the flame of discontent.

"You see, my dear, most people do everything they can to smother the flame. As we grow up, and as we grow more uncomfortable with discontent, we turn on the television or stream music or play video games. Some will drink whisky or smoke weed or chase tail. And although you will do all of those things, I don't want you to *only* do those things. I want this flame of discontent to shape every decision you make. I want you to seek it out and feed the coals if you feel them growing cold. I want you to maintain the flame.

"And this match, this is the initial spark. Without it, you will never have the initiative you need to begin a thoughtful life."

The mother had raised her boy to be a challenger. It had always been important that he question everyone, especially her. So The Boy With A Moon On His Leg countered his mother with, "But fire destroys. It isn't creative. How can it sustain anything when it needs to consume?"

"Tell me: where are we, my love?" his mother gently asked.

"In the middle of the woods," he said.

"Most trees are terrible bores. When there is a forest fire, most trees will complain about the heat and be devoured by the flames. And, afterward, if the tree has not already been consumed, the tree will die from the inside out because the ground has become too toxic to support life. In this, trees are quite like most people who are discontent, but in a complaining way. Now. Tell me again, my boy, where are we?"

"In the middle of the *redwoods*," her son answered.

"Fire doesn't destroy these redwoods. It opens them up. The heat of the flames ripens the pinecones, and the ash and aftermath in the soil make the ground fertile for the seeds that spill there. It's a creative process that can only be made through fire.

"The redwoods welcome fire. They are nourished by it. And they create the future through it."

The son took the match from his mother and threw it on the cultural kindling, and they watched the fire as it grew into a small and delightful roar.

"A great deal must be given up or taken away during the act of creation," the mother said. "The fire will build. It will create. It will bring new things into being." She took a piece of the campfire and spread it to the limbs of the nearby trees.

"What are you doing?" her son cried out—the question at once an accusation and a dagger, and a poor substitute for a fire extinguisher.

"If you can welcome the flame with a similar kind of acceptance as these redwoods, when the time comes, you'll understand how to destroy in order to create once again."

And, with that, she wove her arm around her son's shoulders and led him out of the forest to sow some flames to find his own.

MOONCAKES

Conception

I call him The Gingerbread Man. He follows me in disguise, in the shape of flies, hovering beneath an unfamiliar ceiling, a ceiling that isn't mine. He's attached to me at the soul looking for some sort of control, manifesting as shadow. Overflowing with physics, with physical resistance to gravity, I see the shape of him on the periphery of my vision as I brace myself for the decision of our collision.

:|:

Gestation

I feel him kick me in the lung, and I have a craving for milk and rabbit meat. When I burn my mouth on the stew, made from the roux I simmered and browned until it was time for the final showdown, my body rocks and starts to split open; down the center. In the din of airplanes and the memories of ravens, he turns over in my belly and knows what my heart sounds like from the inside. He's as nimble as a spoon, and the soft weight of him in my womb whispers of recipes unmade. Shreds of rabbit meat steep in my bowl, steaming and no longer teaming with life.

The stew will be thick as flies and thieves.

:|:

Before

As a little girl, my mother floated into my room the way coffee smells brewing, asked me what I was doing, scavenging for something unseen but not unknown, under the covers, under my bed, inside of books, inside of my head. I told her she had brown eyes like my brother, The Gingerbread Man. She lit a cigarette and it curled her hair. I scared her then, with the mention of the little boy that we did not share.

The Gingerbread Man and his shadow, an eighty-years-long affliction, ended with my great-grandmother on the floor of a kitchen. My great-grandmother: a twelve-year-old married to a grown man. She gave birth twice by age sixteen. I feel naked when I learn this. It's a fact that my five-year-old grandmother never questioned, a fact worn down by innocence and time. The only memory of her mother that survives, of which my grandmother is absolutely certain, is that she found her mother bleeding on the floor of the kitchen. And as the mother lay dying, she told her daughter to never be alone with her uncle and to stay away from coat hangers. My grandmother slept next to her mother, there on the floor, until her mother's brown eyes weren't brown anymore.

Secrets keep slipping into my hands. "It was too much to bear," my mother said. My mother, gold and slender like bananas, with her hair spilling down her back in curtains, smelled of cigarettes and coconut oil. Her Sicilian skin brown by living across the street from the ocean. She was lovely when she rode her bicycle in buttercream skirts and cherry-red beach walkers, her toenails white as mouse skulls against her tanned flesh, the glint of her knees and calves in the sunlight, a tapestry of semi-sweet chocolate hair flaring in the autumn air behind her. My mother confesses that before I was born she had an abortion, and ever since she's seen the distortion that follows me around.

And there he is in the cookbook: a recipe without a name. "He's counting on you to finish the recipe." My eyes are wide, this cookbook harbors a hundred years inside; the binding loose at the spine like oranges and rinds.

: | :

Rebirth

I can trace my face back to Sicily through the lines of my grandmother. We are the same, she and I, the way we both do not smile for photographs. She tells me she sees her mother in me, our eyes not brown, but sad just the same. I kiss my baby's flesh; this baby that I've waited my entire life to see, whose soul used to live on the periphery. His skin is soft, fuzzy with birth, but cool and delicate like a porcelain teacup, harboring a hundred years inside. Even though I know if I lay a hand upon this teacup, it will snap, I clutch my baby anyway. I kiss his tiny baby lips, his skin so smooth and cool it's scary.

The pages of the cookbook pentagram a process more science than fiction: wires, resistors, bread boxes, and, our good ole buddy, 220 Volt—direct from the main line.

He was a recipe without a name.

As I plug the contraption into the wall, a charge of alternating current to jumpstart his little heart, I tell him, since he's no longer the shadowy Gingerbread Man with a disembodied stare, "I change your name to Mooncakes; yours has been a recipe I was born to prepare."

The rabbit meat stew has long gone cold beside my spoon, and I remember this day as the day I gave birth to the moon.

Attached at the soul, he's caught in my own gravitational pull.

THE GIRL WHO GREW AN ORCHESTRA FROM SEEDS SHE SOWED HERSELF

There was a song in her heart even then; even as a child, she knew that she had a kind of magic that she conducted all her own. She dreamed of watercolor adventures and wool felted kisses that she could save in her pocket and carry with her wherever she went. And music, she dreamed of such sweet music. In her heart, she harbored a secret hope of cultivating a grove of trees that could play instruments themselves, giving her time enough to dance to their melody.

One day, a pipe organ followed her home from school, on her heels right to her door, and when she asked her parents if she could give it a good home, her mother and her father shut the door and gently reminded her that there was already enough music in the world. They tried to convince her it would be a waste of her time to play pipe organs when there were more important things to learn, like fluid dynamics and biomedical engineering.

But she kept that secret hope alive in her heart and carried it with her like a felted kiss.

That pipe organ—the very same that followed the girl home like a puppy—planted itself firmly in her yard and breathed in the wind heavily, down to the depths of its chambers, and exhaled music out of its pipes. Oh, sure, the girl's mother was annoyed that it sat in the middle of the front yard so brazenly, for all the neighborhood to see, and on particularly windy nights, the neighbors sometimes complained; but, her mother had dreams of her own, too—of painting porcelain teacups—and she found that her heart was too artful to rip the pipe organ up by the roots. The girl's mother understood how important it was that the pipe organ be allowed to thrive.

There it waited for the day the girl would be ready to make music of her own. While it waited, with its legs planted in such loving ground, the pipe organ's feet slowly turned into roots, and, soon, spring limbs began to bud. Until, finally, the pipe organ turned into a tree.

The pipe organ tree was massive: the size of a small church, or a pack of hippopotami, with pipes as tall as redwoods. Whenever anyone else sat down in front of the instrument—and many people were tempted to trespass her parents' property to sit at the log bench and try their hand at a tune—only the most horrible of noises emanated from deep within the tree's trunks.

Only the girl's fingers properly knew how to breathe wind and life into the keys of the pipe organ tree.

But, one day, when she was at school, being a dutiful daughter, and faithfully learning Euler's equations and flow velocities, the pipe organ tree started to die. And, by the time she was able to come back home and say goodbye, it was too late. She fell to her knees before what had once been a hybrid of tree and instrument. The mighty pipe organ tree had fossilized. And even though she was sad to her core, she refused to cry for the pipe-organ-tree—for it had enjoyed a good life of playing music on windy nights and entertaining the people in town. As she stood up, she found four acorns that it had dropped before it petrified over. She scooped them up and carried them around in her pocket, determined to finally find the perfect place to plant her own grove.

She scoured the country and even went as far as Greece, looking for fertile ground, but settled on California for the sunshine and the stars. And there she planted four little seeds in fertile ground, allowing her own innate magic to nurture those seeds into sprouting by dancing and singing to the seeds until they each germinated in their own time. And, soon, she grew herself a mighty string quartet.

The first was a giant sequoia that thrummed its strings like a cello. The next was an incense cedar in the shape and sound of a violin. Next came the black oak viola. And last, another violin, but as tall as a ponderosa pine.

And there she danced among the grove she grew herself.

There used to be a voice that whispered in her ear that there weas enough music in the world. That voice was not hers. That voice was off-key; and hers was clear, honest, and pure. So, she called that voice on its bullshit and sang it into the ground, and buried it there, like the fertilizer it was.

Because now is the time for the girl to care for the growing ground of her grove, and to take pride in practicing her own particular forms of music.

And what a sweet symphony it will be.

THE MEMORY OF SAND
CAN KEEP YOU SOFT

Did you know that there was a time when The Insomniac was not named as such? It's true that I only tell you things I want you to know, and I only reveal things when necessary, but, now seems to be the time to reveal the truth about the woman you've come to know as The Insomniac.

When she was younger, much younger than she is now, she was called The Girl Who Dreamed Too Much. She was made of soft stuff, like the blinking lights of a city as can only be seen at night on the back of a motorcycle on the Coronado Bridge. She was made of sand, and salt, and the sea, and she never could have imagined living anywhere except across the street from the ocean. Se was born to that place, and Imperial Beach was as much a part of her as the blood that ran in her veins. To take her away from the mermaids and her shark kin would, certainly, be a sentence worse than death—death, at least, would be swift, like in the movies; forgetting was slow, and takes a lifetime.

Her parents moved her away from the ocean, and into a wayward home for vampires in the middle of the foothills—foothills are a forgotten location, made invisible by their liminal space: they are neither mountains, nor forests, but some ghastly combination in between. After moving away from the sea, The Girl Who Dreamed Too Much was often caught in these in-between spaces: between quires and spines, between walls and doorways, between the everyday horrors of vampirism. Her father saw the way her mother lost herself in the nest of waiting vampires. Her father saw how soft her mother's skin and heart both were.

So, her father insisted that the girl toughen up. Her father insisted that she get rough around the edges. That the girl was far too soft, softer even than her mother, and so he attempted to temper the girl like steel, forgetting instead that the girl was made of sand. So, every time he tried to form or sculpt her in his steely image, she simply fell like sand through a sieve. She learned how to let go of forming herself, but also refused to be formed by anyone at all.

Her father had no patience for a rebellion of the mind. He had been prepared for a rebellion of her body; he had expected her to climb out of windows, to experiment with drugs or in the backseats of Camaros. He had been wholly unprepared for the girl to cling to the sea, and the sand, and the way it made her soft. He worried for his daughter, he really did—he had planned on teaching her the ways of the world, but she was wholly uninterested in believing in vampires, despite the wreckage she witnessed in their wake. Her father wished that his daughter would rebel in a way he could understand, in a way he had prepared for. Instead, he made her softness his enemy to vanquish, and, in doing so, he convinced himself that teaching the girl the language of violence was the only way to save her from herself.

So the girl learned how to speak in tongues. She became fluent in the vernacular of belts—a green military belt with dual lined rivets still held a corrugated sway over her person. She learned how to speak in leather—one belt in particular had been embossed with the image of a super hero, and had left its imprint across her spine. She hated wood the most, though, and sometimes raged at trees for no reason other than she knew what it was to be struck with a two by four. She knew what it was to be hit with a paddle; with a baseball bat—it was skinny, she would confess, barely a bat at all, and even a piece of crown molding with the skinny nails still attached. When her father switched to wire coat hangers, so began his experiment with metal. Occasionally, he unscrewed the antenna from his boombox. And, yes, once, her father hit the girl with an iron poker. But just the once; and then it was back to the common speech of hangers pulled into misshapen wire ovals as he loomed over her.

The girl thought if being soft was so bad that her father felt the need to beat it out of her, she decided that being soft was worth holding on to. And so she conjured sand in her mind and allowed her father to leave imprints across her surface.

When she was too old to be beaten without it being noticed, her father finally named her The Girl Who Dreamed Too Much, and he cautioned her that, if she were going to let her skin be soft enough for even vampires, then, under no circumstances, should she allow her dreams to be filled with soft things like nectarines. He said if she wasn't hard against the world, then the vampires were the least of her worries, and the world would sink its teeth right in, too. He said he tried to turn the girl into something the world would choke on. Something with sharp edges.

"Because," he said, "even nectarines rot."

The Girl Who Dreamed Too Much didn't want her dreams to rot. So, she dreamed about locks, and keys, and galaxies contained behind a keyhole instead. She dreamed of the small, everyday apocalypses that people carry in their hearts, and she dreamed of the tonics they could drink down to heal the gaping wounds errant landmines made in their souls. The girl spent so much time dreaming up ways to make other people feel loved that she started sleeping less and less, until, eventually, she didn't sleep at all. And soon, The Girl Who Dreamed Too Much, a name she loved and loathed in equal measure, became known only as The Insomniac, a name that only described her through her dis-ease, through her affliction of sleeplessness.

And, although The Insomniac survived on very little sleep, she still dreamed of Ireland when her head fell upon a pillow at night. She dreamed of a cottage near a silky black stone cliff marbled with plush verdant green. She dreamed of books and the smell of aged paper and leather bindings. She dreamed of typewriter sounds and the mewling of cats. She dreamed of learning the art of solitude near a salty Celtic sea. She dreamed of dreaming things into being, sitting in the cradle of her soul-life, in the Ring of Kerry.

She dreamed of other things, too, like an emerald hedge maze that, once solved, led her to the middle where she met a scientist. The Chemist was working with a microscope, and he had a keyhole on his chest. After he loaded a glass slide into the microscope, he would silently gesture an invitation to look through the eyepiece. But The Insomniac never felt safe enough to look through the microscope when offered. The Insomniac had dreamed this encounter many times, but she knew from her childhood that she needed to always keep at least one eye on her surroundings.

Then one day, The Chemist asked, "What can I do to make you feel safe enough to look through the microscope?"

The Insomniac had never heard his voice, but it felt familiar and deep, and no one had ever asked her such a thing, so she didn't rightly know. "I don't know what safe feels like," The Insomniac admitted, her voice cracking.

Everybody knows that voices are powered by hearts, and, as such, it takes a person of great discipline to align the heart with the mind—to have one believe the veracity of the other enough to not betray the voice communicating the heart's desire, the truth, with wavering tones of speech. So, when The Insomniac's voice cracked, she was taken aback because she had spent so much time assuring herself that, as long as she was never distracted, being "safe" was something she could achieve all on her own. But if she ever wanted to look in microscopes and make discoveries, she would have to free up enough brainspace by weaning herself off her need for hyper-vigilance. She had been preoccupied for so long with feeling safe, she hadn't realized she hadn't known what being "safe" actually meant, or even felt like. But she was sure that it was the thing she wanted most in the world.

"Perhaps if you gave me some room?" The Insomniac suggested.

Without hesitation, The Chemist backed away and gave The Insomniac as much room as she needed to feel safe enough to focus on what was beneath the microscope, instead of focusing on him.

The first time she leaned her forehead into the eyepiece, it was only for a moment—not nearly long enough to actually observe anything of note. Over time, though, and with the generous patience of The Chemist, The Insomniac eventually became confident enough to look through the lens longer and longer, until, eventually, she was actually able see what was on the glass slide.

When she peered through the lens, she saw the nanopillars of a cicada wing. She became enchanted by the pattern as she adjusted the magnification dial to clarify the sight. Its antimicrobial fatty acids meticulously organized into nano-structures were superhydrophobic. This discovery, she realized, had the potential to be replicated in other settings, like hospitals, to prevent the spread of viruses. It was that moment that The Insomniac realized that this is what being safe felt like.

For her, being safe was the ability to focus on discoveries instead of focusing on sudden movements.

And that's how The Insomniac met The Chemist. Years before they actually met, she knew him in her dreams. Same voice. Same microscope by the water. She had always been too afraid to ever utter the dream aloud because there were too many other explanations to explain the dream away. And, being one who doesn't say things she doesn't mean, she worried that saying it out loud might make her wrong one day. But that deep-seeded knowing never fades, in fact, the roots of it only seem to grow deeper in truth over time.

Mostly, though, she worried about destiny, because she didn't believe in it. Charming as the idea of a master watchmaker was—building a clock in the sky, setting the gears in motion, and then walking away—she believed in making her own choices, in building her own clockworks.

So, when she told The Chemist she loved him, she conveniently left out the part about loving him since before she knew him, precisely because she knew it made no sense. But, more importantly, when she told him she loved him, The Insomniac wanted The Chemist to never doubt that she was making a conscious choice in that love. She did not want him to ever wonder if she really loved him, or, if she was simply submitting to an authority higher than her own.

The Insomniac loved The Chemist not only because he reminded her that her own authority was all she ever needed, but he consistently refused to take any authority over her either. Even when she demanded it because it was a pattern to which she had grown accustomed—he loved her enough to want her to be free, even from him.

He loved her enough to allow her to be soft and retain the memory of sand, and she loved him enough to be strong and turn that sand into the prismatic glass of discovery.

TOMORROWLAND

Planner

The mother buys the blueprints at Home Builders Outlet for $15.99. The father will build it. She gives him the plans that night at dinner. The mother tells him that this swing set will be in the backyard. It will be near the oak tree. It's an A-frame design. The father builds it, but not that weekend. The plans languish on the dining room table for eighteen months. The mother smokes cigarettes on the porch. The swing set is framed between the two triangles composing its structure. It will have a triangle playhouse with a blue tarp for a roof. The father builds it in the rain, because it should've been built already. It will be the only thing he'll ever build. The mother knows this. The swing set will smell of pine.

Past

Isn't their daughter a little old for swing sets anyway? The plunk of raindrops on blue tarp. Bloody thumbs. Missing nails. Stars behind eyes at the speed of light. Chain link swings. Easy knots. Soft mud. Reinforce. Concrete. The blueprints are fucked up. They're white. More like a map. Not like blueprints at all. Things are getting weirder. The swing set is no longer a swing set. The father knows this will be the last thing he will give his child before he leaves her mother. He is thinking that this swing set will be the way to throw her mother off the scent of his leaving. Whoever heard of white blueprints? They're more like a map. Topography of the future.

Portal

The swing set is her rocket ship. Things are getting weirder at the speed of night. Pumping knees at 3Gs. Liftoff. Past the Milky Way. Super boost. There are shuttles and planets, miles away, where the sky is no longer blue. Barred and spiral galaxies compose unsung stars. All there needs to be: she and a swing.

EVEN THE SIMULACRUM HEART IS A LONELY HUNTER

When Patia Faucheaux from Genetic Fiduciary Systems called looking for my father, it became an electrical storm kind of day.

"I'm trying to get a hold of Jack Cody. His father, Inmate Number 06222016 just passed, and now Jack has a genetic interest in Eddy County, New Mexico. I've been trying to get ahold of Jack, but I am unsure of his whereabouts for permit distribution."

I responded, "I'm sorry, but my father is dead."

Patia faltered for a moment, "Beggin' your pardon, ma'am." I saw her scrambling on her end of the screen, flipping through actual paper instead of digital files, so no wonder she was flustered. She paused long enough to ask, "Are you saying you're Jack Cody's daughter? Daughter of Jack Cody and..." her voice trailing off implied she was hoping I would fill in my mother's name for her.

"Claire Salván," I said, and the woman's eyes darted at the screen. My mother's name made her nervous—that and the fact that she did not have a record of my mother and father having been married. As a silicate, I'm able to pick up on cues others may not notice and adjust my approach accordingly. "They divorced. A long time ago."

"I guess it makes sense you're listed as the contact for Jack Cody since you're his daughter and all," Patia said. "Even if that's *legally* impossible."

I suspected that Patia was normally very good at her job, and this lapse in information was making her feel embarrassed so she was trying to rationalize what could be happening. So I tried to lighten the mood with a lazy attempt at a joke to let her know that the lack of information didn't reflect poorly on her. "Well, I'm thirty-eight years old, so I guess having a permit first didn't stop him." I felt compassionate toward this woman I'd never met before this call. It was not my intention to make this stranger feel insecure when she was only trying to do her job. I attempted to brush past the awkward silence for her benefit, "Regardless, my dad died. Years ago. So, do I inherit the birth rights? Is that even possible?"

"Well, darlin', I gotta tell ya," Patia tried to ease the tension by chuckling, "according to Jack Cody's Social Security information, there is no record of his death."

"Now who's talking about what's legally impossible?" I attempted to laugh a good-natured laugh in return for hers.

Patia's face got serious then, "No, seriously, darlin'. There's no death certificate on file, in any state, on his record."

"If I can find him, could he sign the genetic rights over to me?"

"Well, honey," Patia said, giving me a good-natured chuckle of her own that let me know she was patronizing me without trying to hurt my feelings, "Lord willin' and the creek don't rise."

Patia's surprise at my existence was not surprising. The government-sanctioned sterilizations of Latinas didn't last long, three presidential terms to be exact—just long enough to ensure that the predicted new racial majority didn't happen. By the time the bill was revoked, the damage had been done to millions of women, who not only had to endure being victimized by the government, but then continue to be victimized every time they were held up as an example of what happens when society has a complete lack of empathy. My mother was one of those women.

After the policy was rescinded, there was talk of reparations. In a culture where corporations can expand and have subsidiaries while humans still need a permit to reproduce, monetary reparations were not going to happen. Americans don't like the idea of enabling "laziness." Instead, the idea of cultural reparations became the new cry for social justice. What if we could design a better person to ensure this never happened again? Science could incrementally shift society away from narcissistic entitlement fueled by American exceptionalism, toward a more empathetic society interested in public service.

Anything to save the soul of our nation while protecting the beating heart of capitalism.

During this time, computational empathy became one of the most popular subject areas of study for graduate students in cognitive developmental robotics. Unfortunately, all the empathy apps and wearable empathy technology just turned the concept into a cultural joke. "Feelers" got magnetic implants in the thenar webspace of their hands between their fingers, and would try to pick up dates by being able to "sense the vibes" of the other person. Americans: the only people in the world capable of reducing empathy to a pick-up artist technique.

It was concluded that the most organic transmission of empathy into society had to be enacted by people themselves. Biohacked humans, specifically installed with "empathy chips," were hailed as the first phase of social reparations. Naturally, as technology evolved and was refined, this led to people like me: silicates specifically designed for social engineering purposes.

The process is not that different from in-vitro fertilization. People like me are usually engineered with the genetic material of both parents; but, since my mother's ovaries had been removed, and my parents did not have a birth permit, the only S-OB/GYN my parents could afford didn't have the technology to manufacture an egg with my mother's genetic material. There's only so much a back alley reproductive neurologist can do.

I was engineered solely from my father's cells, carried to term in my mother's still intact uterus. As a silicon-based human, the density of my cells is higher, which just means they carry more information. After the empathy gene was isolated, geneticists engineered silicate embryos to express that gene in a way carbon-based humans weren't capable of yet. It had its drawbacks.

Having "an abundance of empathy" requires a lot more processing power and memory space than people like my parents had—for instance, it takes an incredible amount of energy and emotional processing to not absorb the political rhetoric calling people like me socialist blenders. Since the gut is lined with a hundred million nerve cells naturally, the reproductive neurologists ensure that we grow a second neural network in our abdominal cavity. Doctors help us manage our neurodiversity with supplemental exabytes of what essentially amounts to hard drive space as we grow. The phrase "trust your gut" is just a little more literal for us silicates.

My dad was an analog enthusiast, and one of his hobbies was restoring antique DVD and VHS players. He often had two copies of his favorite films: one copy to open and watch, and a separate, unopened copy enshrined within a dusty box in the attic. These objects had value that was only preserved if they were collected but never used. His prized possession had been a DVD copy of *Reservoir Dogs* (in mint condition) that had been given to him by his grandfather. My dad had always been on the hunt for the VHS version. He said if he ever found one, he'd pass it on to me the way his grandfather had passed it on to him.

His obsession with physical objects was likely due to the fact that he wasn't allowed to have many possessions growing up. He came by his skewed object constancy honestly. His family moved around a lot, from Alaska to Louisiana, eventually ending up in California being raised by his grandparents. All of his relatives were either dead or in prison by the time I was born.

Through all the chaos of his childhood though, there were movies, and the thing he wanted to be the most in the world was a filmmaker. He wanted to make movies the original way, with actual film that he could process and splice himself. He used to say that all you needed to make a movie was film that came in a can and a real character to bring it to life. My father and I had been in a diner once and we watched this guy squeeze out a line of ketchup on a single fry. This man ate his whole plate of fries this way. The loneliness and obsession emanating from this man was clear to my augmented brain, but my father viewed it as a simple character quirk. He said that he'd work this character into a real movie someday. He told everyone that the scene would be as famous as the scene at the coffee shop in *Reservoir Dogs*. Except it wouldn't be about Madonna and tipping. It'd be about ketchup. And it'd be made on honest-to-goodness film.

I ran the probability of my father having come across my mother's death notice in a newsfeed; I also ran the odds on him wanting to be found: neither were outlandish.

While my mother was alive, asking her about my father felt like a series of short-circuited betrayals. I'm designed to be sensitive to what scientists call causative electric currents. So, when I would ask my mother about our life with him, her doe-brown eyes would narrow, and the air perceptibly changed around her. Electricity may be the primary organizing force of the universe, but every time I said his name, it was as if there was a sudden, and violent, blackout.

"I'll tell you when you're older."

"When is that?"

My mom would take a long drag on her cigarette and reply, careful not to exhale as she spoke. "Later," she would say. When she did this, the pitch of her voice would drop to 160Hz, and I would be reminded of thunder rumbling in the distance.

"When I grow up and have a kid—"

"I hope they grow up to be just. Like. You."

Flash. Crack. Blackout.

I learned to read her tone and stop asking.

In order to avoid causing emotional blackouts with my mother, I would research my father online to assuage my curiosity from time to time, but I never said a word about it. I knew about the eBook scams he ran. And the spam pages that clogged up old Boolean searches? He was part of that particular problem.

I saved the interesting things I found, like how he was trying to sell rattlesnake venom on a herpetologist message board one time. My father: the literal snake oil salesman.

I never told my mom, though, because I was embarrassed that I wanted to feel close to the man who had run away.

Then, one day, I found a death notice for my father and a short obituary. Car accident. He was fifty-three years old. Dead, alone, unclaimed. No service. No next of kin.

Considering that I am composed of *only* my dad's genetic material, reading that "no next of kin" part felt like what I imagine getting cold-cocked by a Glock after a diamond heist and bleeding out in a backseat must feel like. After that, I never searched for him again. I assumed there'd be nothing to find.

After Patia's call, I quickly fell into my old routing. When I found my father's profile on DreamHost, I felt a plumerial bloom of oxytocin flood my neural pathways. I also tasted pennies.

My father tagged himself a filmmaker living in Las Cruces, New Mexico—regardless of the fact that he had never made a movie that was screened anywhere. He managed to convince a couple DreamHosters that he knew enough about making movies to have appeared on their local, independent livestream last week. His profile said he didn't consider himself an actor, but that he was "looking for some actors to possibly act in some short films for credit and copy. No pay."

It occurred to me that my father was so used to inanimate objects, he forgot how not to treat people as things. I may not be biologically capable of dehumanizing people to exploit them the way he could, but a blender could try.

I signed up for a free DreamHost account. I wanted that birth permit. But I wanted him to want to give it to me. So, I sent the following message to my father:

○ ○ ○

From: "Priscilla Haraway"
To: "Jack Cody"

I saw your profile and I remembered hearing you on Gilla Valley Mornings with Vince & Mel earlier this year. I thought you were really articulate about character development. I particularly enjoyed the bit about finding one personality quirk that translates the essence of a character to the screen. Your example of an anxious, domineering personality selecting one French fry at a time, and individually laying a strip of ketchup along the length was brilliant. Are you still looking for actors? I'm looking to add footage to my reel.

--Priscilla Haraway

I have one photograph of my father. It's actually of the both of us. It's a physical photograph printed on glossy paper that has lost its sheen. The picture is folded in half, permanently creased. It's a side profile of me in my Halloween costume. I'm dressed as Pris from *Blade Runner* and my dad is standing behind me, both of us admiring my reflection in the mirror. The picture has been folded to crop the top of my father's image out.

When I was nine, my mother spent weeks sewing me a princess gown because she wanted me to be Cinderella for Halloween. She had been saving up scraps all year to have enough material for a beautiful dress. But I didn't want to be Cinderella, I wanted to be a replicant for Halloween. I complained about it so often that my mom eventually told me that if I still didn't want to be Cinderella after seeing the finished dress, I didn't have to wear it. Even though I knew how hard my mother worked on the Cinderella dress, I said I didn't want to wear it. Instead of a custom made gown, I pulled old clothes to piecemeal a Pris costume together: beige bodysuit, crimped blonde wig cropped cyborg short. In my heart, I knew I wasn't Cinderella. I wasn't a princess; I was a replicant. Just like Pris.

My father took charcoal out of the woodstove and smudged it across my eyes, and he gave me his black leather jacket to wear even though it went almost to my knees. I felt special because it was one of his favorite analog possessions.

I had chosen my Pris costume, fair and square. I may be engineered for empathy, but I've never been a pushover. Before heading out for trick-or-treating, my mother took a pair of scissors and cut the jacket off of me, and then shredded the jacket to pieces. It wasn't the emotional violence of the thing that haunted me; it was my mother's silence while she did it.

○ ○ ○

From: "Jack Cody"
To: "Priscilla Haraway"

Fellow Night Owl,

I'm in the middle of a project right now, but am always looking for people to fit into future projects. Send me a headshot and your resume.

Jack

My feathered nerves were electrified with the statistical probability that my father not only wanted to be found, but there was the distinct possibility he knew the letter was from me. The way he addressed the letter felt like he was talking to an old friend, and I couldn't ignore the fact that he had chosen "owl" as the nickname—a word so close to my own name, Olivia.

Before he left, he had been working on a movie he wrote, using Super 8 film. My father did everything himself: he wrote, produced, directed, and even managed to record himself as an actor in it. I always asked to go along on the shoots, but my dad always said no. Until one day, my dad said I could be his cinematographer for the day.

I was holding the camera when the woman came by to card us. My father made me give the woman my middle school barcode to scan. She kneeled down next to me and explained that I needed a permit to film in the park, but, just this once, she wasn't going to give me a ticket because I hadn't known any better. She eyed my father while she said this. My father gave me the camera to shoot some establishing shots while he talked to the officer.

From then on, my father always took me filming.

After a week of shooting every single day, my mother and my father argued about how much money he was spending on the movie, while still having nothing to show for it. I saw the argument was escalating, so I tried to diffuse the situation, interjecting that we had been saving a lot of money. In fact, there was an officer who hadn't given us a ticket for filming without a permit. Then I detailed how she continued to help us film until the permit was processed, and all we had to do was use her house as one of the filming locations. I got the establishing shots outside, and Dad got the ones inside.

My mother pulled a knife from the butcher block and turned it on him. My dad jerked me in front of him, hiding behind me. I couldn't have anticipated such a sequence of events.

When it was clear that my father was going to continue to use me as a shield, my mother dropped the knife on the kitchen floor and walked away.

My father never finished the movie.

This ghost of a memory is now superimposed with the truth I failed to pick up on at the time. My father didn't know how to make a movie any better than he knew how to make a family.

○ ○ ○

From: "Priscilla Haraway"

Enclosed, please find my headshot and resume. I was curious what your favorite film was? Mine is *Reservoir Dogs*. I think a person's favorite movie can say a lot about them, and so I hope it speaks for me. It could be indicative of the chemistry we will have.

--Night Owl

Reservoir Dogs. I almost deleted it before sending, but I didn't. *"Every nerve-ending. All my senses. Blood in my veins."* I was Mr. Orange in this game we were playing. O for orange, owl, and Olivia.

Everything was screaming: can he smell the truth? Can he smell it on me? It really seemed like it when he replied.

○ ○ ○

From: "Jack Cody"

Such a pretty bird.

Reservoir Dogs. You got good taste, kiddo. It's my favorite film of all time. Finally managed to get my hands on an actual VHS release of it a while back.

I think I may have a part for you in my next project. Of course, I'll need to have you read for the part first, to see if it's a good fit. When can we meet?

Jack

My favorite conversation I ever had with my mother went like this.

"I think there's a flaw in my code," I said.

"Whaddya mean?" she asked.

"I chase people who run away, instead of appreciating the people that stay," I said.

"Do you know why?" she asked while she lit a cigarette.

"I feel like I'm afraid. I'm afraid I'm not worthy of love because I'm not entirely human."

"Ha!" my mother rolled her eyes at me, "Who is?"

I looked at her something akin to aghast.

"I wear glasses, am I human?" her voice was thick with sarcasm the way molasses is thick.

I rolled my eyes back at her. We were vying for who-could-care-less. "Sometimes, I guess."

"How about people who need medication to live, like insulin? How about babies born with IVF?"

"Of course."

"Are people with pacemakers human?"

"Yes."

My mother smirked to herself as she took a drag on her cigarette. "How about people who use a bionic limb?"

"…Yeeeeeeees."

My mother took a long drag on her cigarette and blew it out slowly, "Then *what* are you talking about?"

I flinched because I could feel the power surge gathering energy for a full-on blackout.

"He left," I said.

○ ○ ○

From: "Priscilla Haraway"

I guess we're both suckers for Tarantino. I should add *Kill Bill* to my list of favorites.

Do you know the Gilla Valley Kitchen on Saguaro? How about we have lunch there on Saturday? They have the best red chilies.

--N. Owl

"Who left?"

"Dad."

"Oh. Riiiiiiiiiight," my mom took a beat, and snuffed out her cigarette on the porch stairs we sat on while we talked. "You think he left because you're silicate?"

"I dunno," I lied.

I never lie.

My mom always knew how to be quiet, and not feel pressured to fill in the silence. It was a skill I always tried to master, but my empathy pathways were paved with constant emotional temperature taking—filling the silence felt like trying to rescue the other person from discomfort, when really it was about trying to quiet my own neural noise. There's empathy and there's projecting, and I cognitively knew the difference, but being programmed to read, adjust, and anticipate the needs of others the way I was, the differences became so murky over time until there was no difference at all.

"We never really have talked about him. Seemed like you didn't want to, and I wanted to respect that," she said.

I finally felt brave enough to admit the ridiculous truth of my worst fear. "He seemed obsessed with old-fashioned technology. I'm the opposite of that. Maybe he wanted a kid born the old-fashioned way."

My mom let out a full belly laugh.

"Please don't laugh."

115

"I'm so sorry—" She put up a hand as if to ask me to hold a moment while she composed herself. "Old fashioned. Newfangled. Didn't matter. He was going to find a way to leave a legacy." She took my face in her calloused hands, rough with whatever work she could cobble together. "He wanted a child. Don't you worry about that."

"Then why did he leave?"

○ ○ ○

From: "Jack Cody"

Kill Bill is a shitty film. It's a chick flick in revenge film's clothing. Shame on you for such poor taste.

What time on Saturday?

My mother laughed, a kind of short and weathered laugh that wasn't meant indicate the lightheartedness of the situation. It was a hard kind of laugh. A 160Hz kind of laugh.

"It's possible the reproductive neurologist we went to might have fucked up your brain chemistry. But. Ya know? You come by it honestly. So maybe it wasn't the doctor's fault so much as it was your dad's fault."

"Please stop," I said. "You blame him for everything," my mother started to protest, "Which is fair—to an extent!" I acknowledged. "But badmouthing his brain chemistry only serves to remind me that I've inherited his defects. So, could you not?"

She stopped when I asked, and mused for a moment before replying, "You always were pretty good at making sure people made more deposits than they made withdrawals. Way better at it than me." She was quiet for a bit, took a deep breath, and said, "Okay. Let's circle back to the Cinderella dress."

I dug the heels of my palms into my eye sockets and rubbed until I saw static, "For fuck's sake."

○ ○ ○

From: "Priscilla Haraway"

How about noon on Saturday?

And, sure, your voice is like honey on the livefeed, but how will I recognize you? Planning on wearing a honey bear 'round your neck?

And *Kill Bill* is not a shitty film. It is the most elaborate love letter ever written.

--Owl

"Do you know why I wanted you to be Cinderella on Halloween that year?"

"I dunno," I sighed, and then I took a stab at it. "You were tired of me rejecting traditional femininity as a child and wanted to doll me up?"

"Not even close," she said. "Does it ever make you feel better when you're wrong?"

The genuineness of her voice when she asked confused me for a moment.

"What?"

"I dunno," she leaned back and mused. "Maybe, for you, being wrong might actually help prove that you are more human than you give yourself credit for."

○ ○ ○

From: "Jack Cody"

You think of everything. Enclosed you'll find *my* headshot. It's not as pretty as yours, but it'll have to do.

P.S. Noon works.
P.P.S. *Kill Bill* is most definitely not a love letter.

"Look," my mother continued, "the world is going to try to convince you that you're only valuable for one thing: what you can produce. But what happens when you can't do that one thing?"

"You find another thing?" I guessed.

"No," she said. "You learn to cherish what you've got. What did Cinderella do in that movie with those discarded scraps? She made a dress with what she had, and she loved it."

"But I wasn't making the dress. You were."

"That's right. For once, I wanted to be the fairy godmother. I wanted to help you learn how to cherish the things you have right in front of you. Instead of, you know, getting caught up in all the things you don't."

She didn't say "like your father" but it echoed in my mind anyway.

"All this time, I had assumed that the Cinderella fiasco was about how I didn't want to wear dresses as a kid."

"Nope."

Since my body is silicon-based, my spine is dense with the extra data it has to process, and I finally understood that all my mom wanted was to be able to turn my pumpkin into a carriage, just once, and she felt rejected when I didn't appreciate the magic she had wrought with her bare hands.

Tears started welling in my eyes, and my voice cracked with emotion against my will. "You could have just told me that," I said, starting to reach out to her.

"Well. There's another reason, too," she said.

From: "Priscilla Haraway"

It is, too, a love letter: Q & U came up with the story together, and then ended up spending the rest of their lives together.

--Priscilla

"I didn't want you to be Pris," she said.

It was my turn to scoff.

"Lemme finish, Olivia," my mother said, holding up her hand, and the frequency of her tone imprinted her seriousness in my mind. "I have never known someone who has the capacity for empathy as you do. It's damn near psychic—so I think it does you good to learn you're wrong from time to time. But part of that empath gift of yours? Your love is as close to unconditional as possible and without judgment, and you don't even expect reciprocation."

"Yeah, but maybe that's could be because I'm silicate."

"It could be the way you're designed. Maybe. We don't know for sure. But, what I do know is: your capacity for empathy doesn't have to be a weakness. It can be your superpower."

"It feels like more than a weakness."

"There. Right there," she pointed at me as she said it. "That's why I didn't want you to be Pris for Halloween back then," she said. "I wanted more for you than to see yourself in a similar story: designed to be exploited. The world will try to dehumanize you enough as it is!" She put her arm around me and pulled me close, "I wanted to teach you that there's a way to protect yourself."

"How? It feels impossible sometimes."

"You can turn that capacity for love on yourself," she said.

While I waited for my dad to respond to my previous message, it felt like I was being disloyal to my mom. I tried to take solace in the fact that I was not chasing my father because my mother was dead. I was not trying to fill a void left behind by the shape of her loss.

I wasn't blind. I just got blood in my eye. And it was time to get to work.

From: "Jack Cody"

Actually, it's an old Hollywood myth that they ended up together. They didn't actually last. But I wouldn't say no to a mint-condition DVD release of *Kill Bill*, especially since I never got around to acquiring it. On account of it being a chick flick and all.

When I arrived at Gilla Valley Kitchen, I chose a booth with red seats in the far most corner. I sat facing the door and submitted my order on the AR display. I wore a disguise, not unlike Pris from *Blade Runner*: beige turtleneck, punky blonde wig, black eyeshadow.

Every time the door opened, my stomach flipped with the rising levels of cortisol in my body. The waitress brought me a plate of fries. I laid a single line of ketchup on each individual fry as I ate.

My father, more grizzled and heavier than the picture he sent, entered the Gilla Valley Kitchen. He wore a grey fleece and cargo shorts. His beard was calico and grey. He wore sunglasses. Ray-Ban, and I knew instantly they were the ones that he used to wear when I was a kid. They were still in excellent condition because he did things like never use the bottom of his shirt to wipe the lenses.

He moseyed in twenty minutes late. After glancing around the diner, not even looking at me, he sat down two tables away. His back was toward me while he faced the door the way I was. He didn't submit an order, so a waitress checked on him. He politely waved her away. The waitress came back with a Pepsi, and asked him if he was ready to order, but he said he was waiting for a friend.

He called me a friend.

If organic aortic pumps could skip a beat, mine surely would have.

I noted the Johnny Cash song that filled the restaurant. I remembered the anecdote my father would always tell when he heard a Johnny Cash song. It felt like all the electricity in the universe was organizing this perfect moment where my dad would reenter my life. I calculated the probability of the things he'd say to me when I went up and introduced myself. "Well, damn, you're so late, Owl, I had to get started without ya. I realize how it is, bein' up all hours workin', though. So don't worry, no hard feelin's. The meal's on me. Did you hear that Johnny Cash song? Did I ever tell you about the time—"

The odds emboldened me to slide out of my seat, and walk the few steps to his table, and clear my throat.

He turned around. He looked me in the eyes. At least I think he did. He had been sitting there with his Ray-Bans still on.

"Are you done with your ketchup?"

"Go nuts, kiddo," he said. His frequency and cadence suggested disappointment, but he hid it behind the sunglasses. He looked out the window as I picked up his ketchup bottle. His avoidance suggested anxiousness. I could sense the electrical current of his heartbeat as I borrowed the ketchup bottle.

I felt a secret thrill as I went back to my table. I hadn't been called kiddo since he left! Was this a signal? This had to be the signal. What was I waiting for?

I turned back around and started to call out, but my father had already made his way toward the virtual paylocked door. He lifted the Ray-Ban Wayfarers off his eyes for a moment so they could be canned and settle his bill. He looked around one last time. Our eyes met.

Cortisol hit me like a bucket of water. *"First there's the shock of it—BAM— right in the face."* I was standing there drenched in panic. All those people in the diner were looking at me, and they knew, man. They could smell it. They could smell it on me.

Except... he didn't.

He didn't recognize me. He walked out the door.

I wanted to stand up and run after him, but my mother's last words echoed in my mind and pinned me to my seat.

"Turn that love on yourself."

In that moment of interaction with my father, I have never been so thankful to be enabled with my abilities.

I had been looking to reconnect with my father, the man who had smeared wood stove ashes across my eyes and helped me cultivate my taste in movies. I wanted the birth permit, yes. But there was a part of me that wanted to catch up on the years we had lost.

Jack Cody, though, had just been looking for a fuck.

○ ○ ○

From: "Jack Cody"
Subject: Re: Gilla Valley Kitchen

I waited for you today, but you never showed. Where were you? If you're not serious about acting, then perhaps we shouldn't work together.

I heard a Johnny Cash song as I waited. I thought of Tarantino movies. If you had been there, I would have told you that my great-granddad saw Johnny Cash at San Quentin in '69.

When I began attending school, my father forbade me from ever giving out our phone number or address to anyone, including kids from school; my father was paranoid that someone would find out that my parents had me without a birth permit. One Sunday afternoon, my mother and I had stopped by the last known 7-Eleven in the United States, a point of pride for our rural community. A girl from my class asked me if I wanted to walk to school with her the next day. I desperately wanted a friend, and I could tell, based on her vocal frequency, that Nicole had wanted to invite me to walk to school for a while, and had only just gathered up the courage to do so. So, when the eight-year-old asked me where I lived, I made a quickly calculated decision. I felt confident that I could appease both my father and my potential friend simultaneously by giving her the intimate detail of my address in exchange for her phone number—a small token that her gesture of friendship was not unappreciated by me. I told her, "I will have to ask my dad for permission. If I don't call you tonight, do not come to my house tomorrow. Because if I don't call, it means I'm not allowed to go with you."

The next morning, Nicole showed up at our door ready to walk to school with me, violating the deal, the terms of which I thought had been clear because I had strategically not called. I had already planned what I'd say when I saw her at school that morning, "Sorry I didn't call, my dad said no, but you already know that."

The knock at the door was the most terrifying and unpredictable thing I could have imagined hearing that morning. Had I not been clear with the girl? Why hadn't she followed my instructions? And what is my dad going to do to her?

When my father saw my classmate at the door, he opened the door only wide enough that he was visible, but he held up a hand to signal me to be quiet while he talked. He was so charming, I was instantly relieved that this was all a misunderstanding. He thanked the little girl for stopping by, but told her I was sick, and wouldn't be in class that day. Better run along. Don't want to be late. It was a long walk after all.

He proceeded to beat me for the next four hours. My body was bruised everywhere that school clothes could cover, and even in a couple places school clothes could not. Back then, those beatings were a common occurrence. Knowing what I know now, no wonder so much of my bandwidth was consumed by thinking about my father. I was constantly trying to be close enough to him to read his moods, and, on the difficult days, coax higher the probability of a remora-like protection from the man-eating shark.

This is a memory I will not miss.

It will never be okay that my father beat me; but, I would have liked to tell him that my heart ached for him. I would have liked to tell him that I wish he had the privilege of having access to the knowledge he needed to make movies as a career, as opposed to working jobs where he had been supremely unhappy. I would have liked to tell him that I wish my mother had been more supportive of his filmmaking, as opposed to taking out her frustration on him about her lack of boundaries.

Most of all, though, I would have liked to tell him that I wish he had been loved the way he needed to be loved as a child, and that I wish his object constancy had developed enough back then so that I could feel safe enough to be his daughter today.

It could have been an opening, an invitation, an olive branch. But the odds of him exploiting my desire to have him back in my life, compounded with the knowledge of my mother's death, were too astronomical to ignore.

I decided then and there that I was designed for empathy, not exploitation. So, instead, I sent him the lyrics of the song that played in the diner. That way at least he'd know I had shown up. That way, at least, there was a statistical chance that he'd finally know it was me.

○ ○ ○

From: "Priscilla Haraway"
Subject: "She Taught Me to Love Her"

Verse One:
I held my daughter,
There in my arms.
Wish I had money,
To keep her from harm
Games are amusin',
That's what they say.
I'm always losin',
Ain't that always the way?

Chorus:
Thinking 'bout my youth now that I'm old.
My thievin' heart has grown so very cold.
I lay on the ground and look at the sky,
And wait for these years to slowly go by.

Verse Two:
Broken heart,
Turbulent mind.
Scattered pictures of a child,
I had to leave behind.
It wasn't right,
Should never have left.
Don't know how I will,
Repay my daughter that debt.

Chorus:
Thinking 'bout my youth now that I'm old.
Love never dies, but hearts can grow cold.
I lay down a blanket and look at the sky,
Hope my kid knows that I love her 'til the day that I die.

A few days later, a box arrived. Inside was a VHS copy of *Reservoir Dogs*—still in the original shrink wrap—and, underneath, the genetic rights to a birth permit signed over to me from my father. No note. No return address. No next of kin to claim.

Before he left, when we were out as a family, people would look at my father, and then at me, and say, "There's no denying her." We were both white and had the same blue eyes and wide jaws, except mine came to a heart-like point. No one ever said that about my mother and me. I used to wish people could see into our hearts so they'd be obligated to say, "There's no denying her."

When I think about my mom, I hope she was able to read me the way I have been able to read everyone—except her. I hope she knew how sorry I was that I didn't choose the Cinderella dress she sewed herself. I hope she knew I was sorry that I hadn't given her bandwidth the way I had given it to my father. I wanted her to know that if I could do it over again, I would have chosen the silver dress she spent weeks sewing.

But I never said any of it. I wanted to wait until I could say it properly. I wanted to make a film only she would see, comprised of all my memories of our lives together housed at the base of my dense spine.

I wanted to prove to her that I finally understood being able to appreciate the things right in front of me.

But she died.

In order to make space for the baby to grow in my womb, some of the exabytes of memory information must be physically removed from the base of my spine that partially fill my abdominal cavity. I don't think I will regret giving up the memories of how I got here. When I finally look at my daughter in my arms, I won't miss the bandwidth memories of my father were taking up in my life. But these memories will still be retrievable; someday, it will be important that my daughter understand that she comes by her empathy honestly.

After I sold *Reservoir Dogs*, that most prized possession, I had the money to hire a reproductive neurologist capable of incorporating enough alleles of my mother's genetic information so that my daughter has an honest-to-goodness grandmother.

And, now, people can look at my daughter and me, and not just into our hearts, to know there's no denying her.

WHEN THE HOUSE FELL DOWN

Before The Insomniac fell in love with The Baker, she had started building a house for herself. It was made of practical things like notebooks and ballpoint pens, cast iron skillets, spatulas, and calendars. There were candles and cakes of watercolors and glue. She fashioned windows out of glass she blew herself, made from the dreamsand of her childhood. But it was of the foundation that made The Insomniac most proud. It was carefully built out of books. She had collected and curated and carefully arranged all the books she ever thought she'd need to build herself a practical little cottage.

Lining the foundation was Emerson, and his treatise on "Self-Reliance" had been dog-eared to remind her that in order to love someone else, she first had to love herself. Next came the collected works of Shakespeare, but she had purchased a special single copy of *Much Ado About Nothing* to emphasize the lessons there—that changing one's mind is not impossible, and does not necessarily have to suggest that the person has fundamentally changed themselves. A much-loved copy of *Weetzie Bat* strategically occupied the space next to *The Girl in the Flammable Skirt* and *Kabuki: Circle of Blood*—all three served as invocations for her spirit, which she knew would be important to hold onto, for she didn't want to lose herself in loving someone else. Edgar Allan Poe's poems and short stories filled in the gaps of the foundation like mortar—for The Insomniac had always suspected that her soulmate had died at least a hundred-fifty years before she had even been born; and, so, she wanted to be reminded that soulmates could be found in places beyond books. And, similar to any good Poe story, soulmates require work unearthing and shine brightest when given the time and attention to learn the secrets that close reading might yield.

Before the house was completed though, The Baker insisted on moving in. The Insomniac protested. Moving in before the house was finished was a curse just waiting to happen, she said. The Insomniac wanted to be proud of the structure she was building; she wanted to be sure of its stability. She wanted to make sure the place was livable, survivable.

But, most of all, The Insomniac wanted to be the one to invite The Baker to live with her in the house she built herself.

Every time The Baker brought up the subject of moving in, he left another box in The Insomniac's under-construction-home. When she insisted he take his boxes with him as he left, The Baker said the boxes were too heavy and he'd take them back next time. When The Insomniac told him that she was worried he was leaving his boxes on purpose, he insisted he was not. When she said his boxes were in the way of the work she needed to do, The Baker said just make the house bigger. When The Insomniac said his boxes were making it impossible for her to think or breathe, The Baker threw a sheet over them and said, "Out of sight, out of mind."

Eventually, The Baker left so many boxes inside The Insomniac's house that, one day, she realized The Baker had managed to move in without her permission. This would not stand. She marched up to him and put her hands on either side of his face and made him look her in the eyes. Had she not been clear, she asked him? Why had he not listened to her? The Insomniac was so confused because, on the one hand, The Baker was her dearest friend, and at being her friend, he excelled in all areas, save this one. She couldn't understand why he refused to respect that her house was her one sacred boundary. She simply could not understand why he couldn't wait for her to invite him to move in—she desperately wanted to want that one day. Just not today. It seemed to her that a real friend would understand her need to build a structure herself, and respect her desire to ultimately invite him to live with her there.

The Baker was equally confused. The Insomniac loved him, yes? She said of course. The Insomniac eventually wanted him to live in this house, yes? Hopefully, she answered. So, The Baker argued, why not now?

The Insomniac pointed at the foundation—still exposed and warping with the weight of all of his boxes. "Because the house is not ready," she insisted. Her voice was filled with broken records, her eyes with heartache, and her actual heart was a naked dandelion stem, the seeds having been blown away through no fault of their own.

"Well," he said, examining the unevenness of the foundation, "why didn't you say so earlier?"

"I did!" The Insomniac said. "Over and again. A thousand times, I said this."

"You mean you didn't want me to give you reasons why it just made sense for me to leave my boxes?"

"No means no," The Insomniac said. "I don't know how to say it more plainly than that. It's why I've always hated your boxes being here at all. It's why I always insist you take them with you, and am angry that you never do. You're clearly not listening to me, but I have too much respect for you and your property to move your boxes to the lawn where they belong. And now look," she pointed at the floor beneath their feet, "I have to create new base supports. Would you please take your boxes and leave? You can come back when it's finished."

The Baker leaned down all the way to the floor, his hands on the covers and spines of the books The Insomniac had architecturally arranged to create the infrastructure. "I don't see the unevenness you see."

"I see it," she said quietly.

"Even if it's there," The Baker stood back up and dusted his hands off on his pants, "it doesn't matter to me. I'll learn to live with it."

"It matters to me," The Insomniac said, she bowed her head and closed her eyes. "And I will never learn to live with it." She opened her eyes and pleaded with her friend, the person she loved most in the world, "Please. Please, just take your boxes. I promise the house will be done soon. And when it is, you can move in."

The Baker was quiet a moment. He looked at the house, nearly finished, with the foundation already crooked, already sinking slightly. He thought about waking up next to The Insomniac in this little house she was building and all he wanted was to help her build it, too. All he wanted to do was let her know that the house was fine just the way it was, and it could always be rebuilt along the way. And that it would go faster with the both of them working on it, anyway.

And in that moment, The Baker decided that he knew what was better for The Insomniac than she knew for herself and said, "No."

To say The Insomniac was devastated by The Baker's refusal would be a gross misrepresentation of her grief. In that moment, The Insomniac's heart disappeared from her chest, having been swallowed up by the black hole that appeared in its place. There was no light that The Insomniac's heart didn't gobble up for breakfast. There was no gravity stronger than the vortex in her soul. That the person she loved and trusted and respected most in the world refused to respect her desires must mean that her desires were so outlandish as to be broken.

Or just plain wrong.

And, so, The Insomniac learned to not trust herself; she learned loving another person meant she wasn't allowed to have an opinion, because her opinions couldn't be trusted.

To characterize the years The Insomniac and The Baker lived together in the unfinished house as unhappy would be to discount all the good they did for each other. One time, The Baker managed to wrestle a chef's knife from The Insomniac when she'd had quite enough of living with a black hole inside her chest. One year, The Insomniac managed to inspire The Baker to chase after his dreams—he had always wanted to change his name to The Chemist, but had been too scared of what changing it would entail. "Baking is really just chemistry anyway," The Chemist said after changing his name. He had said The Insomniac made him brave, and he kissed her forehead in gratitude.

There was a lot of love that filled the house, but not an ounce of trust.

So, even though the years of living there could be said to have been good, those years had never really been happy for The Insomniac, for it is impossible to even recognize happiness when one cannot be trusted to know their own mind.

And, just as she had feared, the house started to disintegrate.

It was slow at first. The foundation was, indeed, uneven, and, everybody knows building walls on an uneven structure is just a curse waiting to happen. The sloped floors bowed the walls, so The Insomniac stuffed angled objects in the seams between walls and floors in a last ditch effort to make the walls less crooked. She tried logic and T-squares and even three different kinds of triangles. But the walls were so warped that the plaster in the ceilings cracked and eventually caved in. For a time, concussions were common and just became a hazard of living in the house. The Insomniac wanted to move, but The Chemist insisted the house was inhabitable, and brought home hardhats for them to wear, instead. "Like nothing ever happened," he said.

The floors twisted the walls until the frail skeleton of the home could be seen from beneath the plaster and dry wall. When the walls split apart and opened up to the outside, bats began to nest in the in-betweens. When The Insomniac tried showing The Chemist the bats roosting there, they were gone quicker than eyesight allowed. They're like faerie creatures that way: you either see them or you don't, and since The Chemist couldn't see them, he surmised the bats didn't exist.

The walls twisted until the glass in the windows started to sing and shriek. The Insomniac tried doing what she could to release the tension on the windowpanes. She tried buttressing them with sashes, and, when that didn't work, she tried drilling tiny holes in the glass to alleviate the pressure. But the glass—the beautifully swirled glass The Insomniac had made from the dreamsands of her childhood—shattered and burst.

The notebooks and canvases and cakes of watercolor, the board games, the stained glass lamps, the flasks of whiskey, pens filled with purple ink, pens filled with black ink, comic books, DVDs, plates bought in Little Tokyo, shot glasses bought at Olvera Street, wool coats, scarves—all of the items that The Insomniac had carefully plastered into the walls to create the house, everything that constructed the house, broke apart.

She told The Chemist to go. "There's nothing left here," she said.

There was nothing left for her to do, either, no renovation left to try, except to allow the house to fall apart.

And, so, the house fell down.

And The Insomniac watched.

And an apocalypse bloomed inside her chest.

After the house finally collapsed, The Insomniac walked through the wreckage, looking for the spot in the floor where she had buried a safe with a combination dial, beneath all the books.

It was where she had saved her hope.

To get to the safe, though, she had to dismantle all the collapsed things in her way. She started taking down the walls that she had built. She had been so proud of these walls once, but, as she tore them down she realized all she had managed to do was keep out the things she wanted to come in.

When she finally reached the safe where her hope was stored, the only combination that'd unlock the mechanism was asking the two most specific questions she could think up.

"Will I ever learn how to let love come in? And will I have the space for it when it does?"

Luckily, the safe didn't operate on answers, only questions, and once it clicked open, The Insomniac managed to reclaim her hope.

Her hope didn't stop up the black hole where her heart should've been.

Her hope didn't heal the apocalypse.

But her hope let her make things again.

And, with it, she started making herself another house.

THANK YOU

All illustrations appearing in this book were custom drawn by Caitlin Cheowanich and are used with her permission. She also illustrated the image that appears on the cover of this book. The flat lay collage on the cover was designed by me, and I'd like to thank Cheyenne, the artist and designer behind Sugarbone, for allowing me to use her enamel pin design "Cousins" on the cover of this book—if you know the *Sailor Moon* reference, then you *know*. You can find more of Cheyenne's work at sugarbones.net and on Patreon where she has a monthly pin club.

This book would not exist without the support and patience of the team at Sundress Publications. Thank you, Erin Elizabeth Smith and Saba Razvi, for believing in this book and bringing it into existence. Thank you to the Sundress team for doing the thankless jobs necessary to finish this project: Tierney Bailey, Anna Black, Kanika Lawton, Kathleen Gullion, Ashley Somwaru, and Mary Sim.

I want to thank my mother, Jean Retherford, for being my first muse. She's my original moon goddess. She taught me how to be resilient without letting the world make me hard. Both she, and my in-laws, Nancy and Thomas Burcar, have helped keep my family afloat through difficult times and I'm so grateful for them all.

Friends can be in your life for a chapter, for a volume, or all the way to the end. Each of the following people, whether we still appear on one another's pages or not, has been important to me as a friend, mentor and muse: Aimee Bender, Betty Bayer, Francesca Lia Block, Neil Aitken, Natasha Alvandi, Jonathan Bellows, Andrea Blythe, Alex Bryce, Michele Burcar (and my niece and nephews Juliana, Maksim and Brady), Stephan Clark, Anna Creadick, Erin Cunningham, Drew Eliza, Joe Fruscione, Dennis and Michele Gleeton, Jazz Hager, Julie and Damon Hawk, Susan Henking, Mary Hess, Kerry Jahn, Tiffany Knoell, Laura Loo (and her husband Lucas Miller, and their children Cecilia, Stan, and Madeleine), Robi Lipscomb, Cathy Lopez, Steve and Heather Lynn, Allie Marini, Bailey Meeker,

César Menor-Salván, Jenny Mercury, Stacy and Michael Moore, Kevin T. Moss, Dr. Nirupama Natarajan, Lindsay Nelson-Santos, Justina Nemoy, Gary Newman, Cat Rambo, Melody Randolph, Saba Razvi, Matthieu Retherford, Hunter Retherford, Loren Rhoads, Daniela Rogers, Jessica Rosepins, A.B. Rutledge, Isaac Schankler, Andrew Schoonmaker, Charlie Shipley, Josie Sibara and Jay, Hannah Smith, Laurel Snyder, Katy Stenta, Jerome Steuart, Gene Tanke, Melanie Terrill, Laura Thorn, Cody Todd, Valerie Valdes, Annie Vincente Manion, Desmond Woolston, Lorie and Josh Witkop, and Christie Yant. And, although I don't know them personally, reading the work of Mystic Medusa, Chani Nicholas, and Clarissa Pinkola Estés have been important cauldrons of inspiration.

I'd like to pay special thanks to three artists whose work and friendship have been especially important to me. Kira Lees is one of the loveliest writers I know (and one of the scrappiest); she generously allowed me to include her character "star mother" in "Cosmic Ice Empress." Caitlin Cheowanich is a brilliant artist whose style combines mythology with ephemerality, and her art and generosity constantly inspire me. Erika Wenstrom is the inspiration behind "The Woman Made of Water," and that story is my love letter to her. She has an ancient kind of wisdom that I don't understand how a mere mortal has attained, and her friendship has been lifesaving and soul-nourishing.

Finally, I'd like to sing about the unsung heroes of this book: my husband, Bradley, and our son, Nikola. Thank you for your kindness, and your patience, and all of your invisible labor that allowed this book to happen. Thank you for helping me create a new normal after my brain injury. Brad, your emotional intelligence and resilience continue to astound and humble me, even after twenty years. Nikola, your creativity and gentleness far exceed my own, and I'm so grateful that I get to learn by watching you grow. And, ya know, thanks for putting up with my more Slytherin tendencies.

It is my promise that I will continue to try my best to deserve you all for the rest of my days.

ABOUT THE AUTHOR

Jilly Dreadful is the author of *The Spectral Dollhouse*, a book-length digital text where readers enact the process of creativity by making connections between the visual and conjuring her writing as ghosts that haunt the space. It is published by *The New River*, which is archived by the Library of Congress for important cultural contributions of digital texts. She also wrote the libretto for *Light & Power: A Tesla/Edison Story*, a chamber opera with music composed by Isaac Schankler, which was performed in Boston by the Juventas New Music Ensemble. Her short stories have been published in *Lightspeed Magazine* and *She Walks In Shadows*, edited by Silvia Moreno-Garcia and Paula R. Stiles. Her work has been nominated for a Pushcart Prize, received honorable mention for best science fiction of the year, and long-listed for best horror of the year by Ellen Datlow.

She completed a Ph.D. in Creative Writing and Literature at University of Southern California, going on to create The Brainery: Online Speculative Fiction Workshops + Resources, which has been featured on *Geek's Guide to the Galaxy*, *Wired.com*, among others.

Dreadful was born in California, but no longer lives there. Her heart aches for it every day, but she's learned to define home as where her husband and son are instead.

jillydreadful.net
@jillydreadful

OTHER SUNDRESS FICTION TITLES

I Am Here to Make Friends
Robert Long Foreman
$20

The Butterfly Lady
Danny M. Hoey, Jr.
$16